Frank M. Lupton

Famous Dramatic Recitations

Frank M. Lupton

Famous Dramatic Recitations

ISBN/EAN: 9783337375362

Printed in Europe, USA, Canada, Australia, Japan

Cover: Foto ©Andreas Hilbeck / pixelio.de

More available books at **www.hansebooks.com**

Famous Dramatic Recitations.

CAREFULLY SELECTED FROM THE WRITINGS OF THE BEST AUTHORS, AS RECITED BY THE LEADING ELOCUTIONISTS OF AMERICA.

THE SWITCHMAN'S CHRISTMAS STORY.

YES, it's a quiet station, but it suits me well
    enough;
I want a bit of the smooth now, for I've had my
    share o' rough.
This berth that the company gave me they gave
    as the work was light:
I was never fit for the signals after one awful
    night.
I'd been on the line from a younker, and I'd never
    felt the strain
Of the lives at my right hand's mercy in every
    passing train.
One day there was something happened, and it
    made my nerves go queer,
And it's all through that as you find me the
    station-master here.

I was on the switch down yonder—that's where
    we turn the mails
And specials and fast expresses on to the centre
    rails;
The side's for the other traffic—the freight and
    the local slows.
It was rare hard work at Christmas—when double
    the traffic grows.
I've been on duty down yonder nigh sixteen
    hours a day,
Till my eyes grew dim and heavy, and my thoughts
    went all astray;
But I've worked the switch half sleeping, and
    once I slept outright,
Till the roar of the Limited woke me, and I nearly
    died with fright.

Then I thought of the lives in peril and what
    might have been their fate
Had I sprung to the points that evening a tenth of
    a tick too late;
And a cold and ghastly shiver ran icily through
    my frame
As I fancied the public clamor, the trial and bitter
    shame.
I could see the bloody wreckage—I could see the
    mangled slain—
And the picture was seared forever, blood-red, on
    my heated brain.
That moment my nerve was shattered, for I
    couldn't shut out the thought
Of the lives I held in my keeping and the ruin
    that might be wrought.

That night in our little cottage, as I kissed our
    sleeping child,
My wife looked up from her sewing, and told me,
    as she smiled,
That Johnny had made his mind up—he'd be a
    switchman too.
"He says when he's big, like daddy, he'll work on
    the line with you."

I frowned, for my heart was heavy, and my wife
    she saw the look;
Lord bless you! my little Alice could read me like
    a book.
I'd to tell her of what had happened, and I said that
    I must leave,
For a switchman's arm ain't trusty when terror
    lurks in his sleeve.

But she cheered me up in a minute, and that night,
    ere we went to sleep,
She made me give her a promise, which I swore
    that I'd always keep—
It was always to do my duty. "Do that, and then,
You'll have no worry," said Alice, "if things go
    well or ill.
There's something that always tells us the things
    that we ought to do "—
My wife was a bit religious and in with the chapel
    crew;
But I knew she was talking reason, and I said to
    myself, says I,
"I won't give in like a coward—it's a scare that'll
    soon go by."

Now, the very next day the missus had to go to
    the market town;
She'd the Christmas things to see to and she
    wanted to buy a gown.
She'd be gone for a spell, for the party didn't come
    back till eight,
And I knew, on a Christmas eve, too, the trains
    would be extra late.
So she settled to leave me Johnny, and then she
    could turn the key—
For she'd have some parcels to carry, and the boy
    would be safe with me.
He was five, was our little Johnny, and quiet and
    nice and good—
He was mad to go with daddy, and I'd often prom-
    ised he should.

It was noon when the missus started—her train
    went by my box;
She could see, as she passed my window, her dar-
    ling's curly locks.
I lifted him up to mammy, and he kissed his l'tle
    hand.
Then sat, like a mouse, in the corner, and thought
    it was fairy land.
But somehow I fell a-thinking of a scene that
    would not fade.
Of how I had slept on duty, until I grew afraid;
For the thought would weigh upon me, one day I
    might come to lie
In a felon's cell for the slaughter of those I had
    doomed to die.

The fit that had come upon me like a hideous
  nightmare seemed,
Till I rubbed my eyes and started like a sleeper
  who has dreamed.
For a time the switch had vanished—I'd worked
  like a mere machine—
My mind had been on the wander, and I'd neither
  heard nor seen.
With a start I thought of Johnny, and I turned the
  boy to seek,
Then I uttered a groan of anguish, for my lips refused to speak;
There had flashed such a scene of horror swift on
  my startled sight
That it curdled my blood in terror and sent my
  red lips white.

It was all in one awful moment—I saw that the
  boy was lost;
He had gone for a toy, I fancied, some child from
  a train had tossed;
The local was easing slowly to stop at the station
  here,
And the Limited Mail was coming, and I had the
  line to clear.
I could hear the roar of the engine—I could almost
  feel its breath,
And right on the centre metals stood my boy in
  the jaws of death;
On came the fierce fiend, tearing straight for the
  centre line,
And the hand that must wreck or save it, O merciful God, was mine!

'Twas a hundred lives or Johnny's. O Heaven!
  what could I do?
Up to God's ear that moment a wild, fierce question flew—
"What shall I do, O Heaven?" and sudden and
  loud and clear
On the wind came the words, "Your duty!" borne
  to my listening ear.
Then I set my teeth, and my breathing was fierce
  and short and quick.
"My boy!" I cried, but he heard not; and then I
  went blind and sick;
The hot, black smoke of the engine came with a
  rush before
I turned the mail to the centre, and by it flew with
  a roar.

Then I sank on my knees in horror, and hid my
  ashen face—
I had given my child to Heaven; his life was a
  hundred's grace.
Had I held my hand a moment, I had hurled the
  flying mail
To shatter the creeping local that stood on the
  other rail!
Where is my boy, my darling! O God, let me hide
  my eyes.
How can I look—his father—on that which there
  mangled lies?
That voice!—O merciful Heaven!—'tis the child's,
  and he calls my name!
I hear, but I cannot see him, for my eyes are filled
  with flame.

I knew no more that night, sir, for I fell as I heard
  the boy;
The place reeled round and I fainted—swooned
  with the sudden joy.
But I heard on the Christmas morning, when I
  woke in my own warm bed,
With Alice's arms around me, and a strange, wild
  dream in my head
That she'd come by the early local, being anxious
  about the lad,
And had seen him there on the metals, and the
  sight nigh drove her mad—

She had seen him just as the engine of the Limited
  closed my view,
And she leaped on the line and saved him just as
  the mail dashed through.

She was back in the train in a second, and both
  were safe and sound—
The moment they stopped as the station she ran
  here, and I was found
With my eyes like a madman's glaring, and my
  face a ghastly white;
I heard the boy and I fainted, and I hadn't my
  wits that night.
Who told me to do my duty? What voice was that
  on the wind?
Was it fancy that brought it to me? or were there
  God's lips behind!
If I hadn't a-done my duty—had I ventured to dis-
  obey—
My bonny boy and his mother might have died by
  my hand that day.

—*George R. Sims.*

GONE WITH A HANDSOMER MAN.

JOHN.

I'VE worked in the field all day, a plowin' the
  "stony streak;"
I've scolded my team till I'm hoarse; I've tramped
  till my legs are weak;
I've choked a dozen swears, (so's not to tell Jane
  fibs,)
When the plow-pint struck a stone and the handles punched my ribs.

I've put my team in the barn, and rubbed their
  sweaty coats;
I've fed 'em a heap of hay and half a bushel of
  oats;
And to see the way they eat makes me like eatin'
  feel,
And Jane won't say to-night that don't make
  out a meal.

Well said! the door is locked! but here she's left
  the key,
Under the step, in a place known only to her and
  me;
I wonder who's dyin' or dead, that she's hustled
  off pellmell;
But here on the table's a note, and probably this
  will tell.

Good God! my wife is gone! my wife is gone
  astray!
The letter it says, "Good-bye, for I'm a going
  away;
I've lived with you six months, John, and so far
  I've been true,
But I'm going away to-day with a handsomer man
  than you."

A han'somer man than me! Why, that ain't much
  to say;
There's han'somer men than me go past here every day.
There's han'somer men than me—I ain't of the
  han'some kind;
But a *loven'er* man than I was, I guess she'll never
  find.

Curse her! curse her! I say, and give my curses
  wings!
May the words of love I've spoken be changed to
  scorpion stings!
Oh, she filled my heart with joy, she emptied my
  heart of doubt,
And now, with a scratch of a pen, she let's my
  heart's blood out!

Curse her! curse her! say I, she'll some time rue
  this day;
She'll some time learn that hate is a game that
  two can play;
And long before she dies she'll grieve she ever
  was born,
And I'll plow her grave with hate, and seed it
  down to scorn.

As sure as the world goes on, there'll come a time
  when she
Will read the devilish heart of that han'somer
  man than me;
And there'll be a time when he will find, as others
  do,
That she who is false to one, can be the same with
  two.

And when her face grows pale, and when her
  eyes grow dim,
And when he is tired of her and she is tired of
  him,
She'll do what she ought to have done, and coolly
  count the cost;
And then she'll see things clear, and know what
  she has lost.

And thoughts that are now asleep will wake up
  in her mind.
And she will mourn and cry for what she has left
  behind;
And maybe she'll sometimes long for me—for me
  —but no!
I've blotted her out of my heart, and I will not
  have it so.

And yet in her girlish heart there was somethin'
  or other she had
That fastened a man to her, and wasn't entirely
  bad;
And she loved me a little, I think, although it
  didn't last;
But I mustn't think of these things—I've buried
  'em in the past.

I'll take my hard words back, nor make a bad
  matter worse;
She'll have trouble enough; she shall not have
  my curse;
But I'll live a life so square—and I well know that
  I can,—
That she always will sorry be that she went with
  that han'somer man.

Ah, here is her kitchen dress! it makes my poor
  eyes blur;
It seems when I look at that, as if 'twas holdin'
  her.
And here are her week-day shoes, and there is her
  week-day hat,
And yonder's her weddin' gown: I wonder she
  didn't take that.

'Twas only this mornin' she came and called me
  her " dearest dear,"
And said I was makin' for her a regular paradise
  here;
O God! if you want a man to sense the pains of
  hell,
Before you pitch him in just keep him in heaven
  a spell!

Good-bye! I wish that death had severed us two
  apart,
You've lost a worshiper here, you've crushed a
  lovin' heart.
I'll worship no woman again; but I .guess I'll
  learn to pray,
And kneel as *you* used to kneel, before you run
  away.

And if I thought I could bring my words on
  Heaven to bear,
And if I thought I had some little influence there,
I would pray that I might be, if it only could be
  so,
As happy and gay as I was a half an hour ago.

JANE (*entering*).

Why, John what a litter here! you've thrown
  things all around!
Come, what's the matter now? and what have you
  lost or found?
And here's my father here, a waiting for supper,
  too;
I've been a riding with him—he's that " handsomer man than you."

Ha! Ha! Pa take a seat, while I put the kettle on.
And get things ready for tea, and kiss my dear
  old John.
Why, John, you look so strange! come, what has
  crossed your track?
I was only a joking you know, I'm willing to take
  it back.

JOHN (*aside*).

Well, now, if this ain't a joke, with rather a bitter
  cream!
It seems as if I'd woke from a mighty ticklish
  dream;
And I think she " smells a rat," for she smiles at
  me so queer,
I hope she don't; good gracious! I hope that they
  didn't hear!

'Twas one of her practical drives, she thought I'd
  understand!
But I'll never break sod again till I get the lay of
  the land.
But one thing's settled with me—to appreciate
  heaven well,
'Tis good for a man to have some fifteen minutes
  of hell.
                                 —*Will Carleton.*

THE DEATH OF THE OLD SQUIRE.

Read with great success by Charlotte Cushman.

'Twas a wild, mad kind of night, as black as the
  bottomless pit;
The wind was howling away like a Bedlamite in
  a fit,
Tearing the ash boughs off, and mowing the poplars down,
In the meadows beyond the old flour mill, where
  you turn off to the town.

And the rain (well, it *did* rain) dashing against
  the window glass,
And deluging on the roof, as the Devil were come
  to pass;
The gutters were running in floods outside the
  stable door,
And the spouts splashed from the tiles, as they
  would never give o'er.

Lor', how the winders rattled! you'd almost ha'
  thought that thieves
Where wrenching at the shutters, while a ceaseless peolt of leaves
Flew to the doors in gusts; and I could hear the
  beck
Falling so loud I knew at once it was up to a tall
  man's neck.

We was huddling in the harness-room by a little scrap of fire,
And Tom, the coachman, he was there, a-practic-ing for the choir.
But it sounded dismal, anthem did, for Squire was dying fast,
And the doctor said, do what he would, Squire's breaking up at last.

The death-watch, sure enough, ticked loud just over th' owd mare's head,
Though he had never once been heard up there since master's boy lay dead;
And the only sound, beside Tom's toon, was the stirring in the stalls,
And the gnawing and the scratching of the rats in the owd walls.

We couldn't hear Death's foot pass by, but we knew that he was near,
And the chill rain and the wind and cold made us all shake with fear;
We listened to the clock up-stairs, 'twas breath-ing soft and low
For the nurse said, at the turn of night the old Squire's soul would go.

Master had been a wildish man, and led a rough-ish life;
Didn't he shoot the Bowton squire, who dared write to his wife?
He beat the Rads at Hindon Town, I heard, in twenty-nine,
When every pail in market-place was brimmed with red port wine.

And as for hunting, bless your soul, why, for forty year or more
He'd kept the Marley hounds, man, as his fayther did afore;
And now to die and in his bed—the season just be-gun—
"It made him fret," the doctor said, "as it might do any one."

And when the sharp young lawyer came to see him sign his will,
Squire made me blow my horn outside as we were going to kill;
And we turned the hounds out in the court—that seemed to do him good;
For he swore, and sent us off to seek a fox in Thornhill Wood.

But then the fever it rose high and he would go see the room
Where mistress died ten years ago when Lammas-tide shall come;
I mind the year, because our mare at Salisbury broke down;
Moreover, the town-hall was burnt at Steeple Dinton Town.

It might be two, or half-past two, the wind seem-ed quite asleep;
Tom, he was off, but I, awake, sat watch and ward to keep;
The moon was up, quite glorious like, the rain no longer fell,
When all at once out clashed and clanged the rusty turret bell.

That hadn't been heard for twenty year, not since the Luddite days.
Tom he leaped up, and I leaped up, for all the house a-blaze
Had more not scared us half so much, and out we ran like mad,
I, Tom and Joe, the whipper-in, and t' little stable lad.

"He's killed himself," that's the idea that come into my head;
I felt as sure as though I saw Squire Barrowly was dead;
When all at once a door flew back, and he met us face to face;
His scarlet coat was on his back, and he looked like the old race.

The nurse was clinging to his knees, and crying like a child;
The maids were sobbing on the stairs, for he look-ed fierce and wild;
"Saddle me Lightning Bess, my men," that's what he said to me:
"The moon is up, we're sure to find at Stop or Etterly.

"Get out the dogs; I'm well to-night, and young again and sound,
I'll have a run once more before they put me un-der ground;
They brought my father home feet first, and it never shall be said
That his son Joe, who rode so straight, died quiet-ly in his bed.

"Brandy!" he cried; "a tumbler full, you women howling there,"
Then clapped the old black velvet cap upon his long gray hair,
Thrust on his boots, snatched down his whip, though he was old and weak;
There was a devil in his eye that would not let me speak.

We loosed the dogs to humor him, and sounded on the horn;
The moon was up above the woods, just east of Haggard Bourne.
I buckled Lightning's throat-lash fast; the Squire was watching me;
He let the stirrups down himself so quick, yet carefully.

Then up he got and spurred the mare and, ere I well could mount,
He drove the yard-gate open, man, and called to old Dick Blount,
Our huntsman, dead five years ago—for the fever rose again,
And was spreading like a flood of flame fast up into his brain.

Then off he flew before the dogs, yelling to call us on,
While we stood there, all pale and dumb, scarce knowing he was gone;
We mounted, and below the hill we saw the fox-break out,
And down the covert ride we heard the old Squire's parting shout.

And in the moonlit meadow mist we saw him fly the rail
Beyond the hurdles by the beck, just half way down the vale;
I saw him breast fence after fence—nothing could turn him back;
And in the moonlight after him streamed out the brave old pack.

'Twas like a dream, Tom cried to me, as we rode free and fast,
Hoping to turn him at the brook, that could not well be passed,
For it was swollen with the rain; but ah, 'twas not to be:
Nothing could stop old Lightning Bess but the broad breast of the sea.

The hounds swept on, and well in front the mare
  had got her stride;
She broke across the fallow land that runs by the
  down side.
We pulled up on Chalk Linton Hill, and, as we
  stood us there,
Two fields beyond we saw the Squire fall stone
  dead from the mare.

Then she swept on, and in full cry the hounds went
  out of sight;
A cloud came over the broad moon and something
  dimmed our sight.
As Tom and I bore master home, both speaking under breath;
And that's the way I saw th' owd Squire ride
  boldly to his death.

                  —*Anon.*

POOR-HOUSE NAN.

DID you say you wished to see me sir! Step in;
  'tis a cheerless place,
But you're heartily welcome all the same; to be
  poor is no disgrace!
Have I been here long? Oh, yes, sir!—'tis thirty
  winters gone
Since poor Jim took to crooked ways and left me
  all alone!
Jim was my son, and a likelier lad you'd never
  wish to see,
Till evil counsels won his heart and led him away
  from me.

'Tis the old and pitiful story, sir, of the devil's
  winding stair,
And men going down—and down—and down—to
  blackness and despair;
Tossing about like wrecks at sea, with helm and
  anchor lost,
On, and on, through the surging waves, nor caring
  to count the cost;
I doubt sometimes if the Savior sees—he seems so
  far away—
How the souls he loved and died for, are drifting
  —drifting astray.

Indeed, 'tis a little wonder, sir, if woman shrinks
  and cries,
When the life-blood on Rum's altar spilled is
  calling to the skies!
Small wonder if her own heart feels each sacri-
  ficial blow,
For isn't each life a part of hers? each pain her
  hurt and woe?
Read all records of crime and shame—'tis bitterly,
  sadly true;
Where manliness and honor die, there some
  woman's heart dies too!

Often I think, when I hear folks talk so prettily
  and so fine,
Of "Alcohol as a needful food;" of "the moderate use of wine;"
How "the world couldn't do without it, there was
  clearly no other way,
But for man to drink, or let it alone, as his own
  strong will might say;"
That "to use it but not abuse it was the proper
  thing to do;"
How I wish they'd let old Poor House Nan preach
  her little sermon too!

I would give them scenes in a woman's life that
  would make their pulses stir,
For I was a drunkard's child and wife—aye, a
  drunkard's mother, sir!
I would tell of childish terrors, of childish tears
  and pain;
Of cruel blows from a father's hand, when rum
  had crazed his brain;

He always said he could drink his fill, or let it
  alone as well;
Perhaps he might; he was killed one night in a
  brawl—in a grog shop-hell!

I would tell of years of loveless toil the drunkard's
  child had passed,
With just one gleam of sunshine, too beautiful to
  last!
When I married Tom I thought for sure I had
  nothing more to fear;
That life would come all right at last—the world
  seemed full of cheer;
But he took to moderate drinking; he allowed
  'twas a harmless thing,
So the arrow sped, and my bird of Hope came
  down with a broken wing!

Tom was only a moderate drinker, ah, sir, do you
  bear in mind
How the plodding tortoise in the race left the
  leaping hare behind?
'Twas because he held right on and on, steady and
  true, if slow;
And that's the way, I'm thinking, that the moderate drinkers go!
Step over step—day after day—with sleepless,
  tireless pace,
While the toper sometimes looks behind and tar-
  ries in the race.

Ah, heavily in the well-worn path poor Tom
  walked, day by day,
For my heartstrings clung about his feet and
  tangled up the way;
The days were dark, and friends were gone, and
  life dragged on full slow;
And children came, like reapers sad to a harvest
  of want and woe!
Two of them died, and I was glad when they lay
  before me dead.
I had grown weary of their cries—their pitiful
  cries for bread!

There came a time when my heart was stone; I
  could neither hope nor pray,
Poor Tom lay out in the potter's field, and my boy
  had gone astray,
My boy who had been my idol; while other hounds
  athirst for blood,
Between my breaking heart and him the liquor
  seller stood
And lured him on with his poisoned words, his
  pleasures and his wine;
Ah, God have pity on other hearts, as bruised and
  hurt as mine.

There were whispers of evil-doing, of dishonor
  and of shame,
That I cannot bear to think of now, and would not
  dare to name!
There was hiding away from the light of day,
  there was creeping about at night,
A hurried word of parting—then a criminal's
  stealthy flight!
His lips were white with remorse and fright when
  he gave me a good-bye kiss!
And I've never seen my poor, lost boy from that
  black day to this!

Ah, none but a mother can tell you, sir, how a
  mother's heart will ache,
With the sorrow that comes of a sinning child,
  with grief for a lost one's sake,
When she knows the feet she trained to walk have
  gone so far astray,
And the lips grow bold with curses, that she
  taught to sing and pray.
A child may fear—a wife may weep, but of all
  sad things, none other
Seems half so sorrowful to me as being a drunkard's mother!

They tell me that down in the vilest dens of the
   city's crime and murk.
There are men with the hearts of angels, doing
   the angels' work;
That they win back the lost and the strayed, that
   they help the weak to stand
By the wonderful power of loving words—and the
   help of God's right hand!
And often and over, the dear Lord knows, I've
   knelt and prayed to him
That somewhere, somehow, 'twould happen that
   they'd find and save my Jim.

You'll say 'tis a poor old woman's whim; but when
   I prayed last night,
Right over yon eastern window there shone a
   wonderful light!
(Leastways it looked that way to me) and out of
   the light there fell
The softest voice I ever heard; it rang like a silver
   bell;
And these were the words: " The prodigal turns
   tired by want and sin.
He seeks his father's open door; he weeps and
   enters in."

Why, sir, you're crying as hard as I; what is it I
   have done?
Have the loving voice and the Helping Hand
   brought back my wandering son?
Did you kiss me and call me " Mother,"—and fold
   me to your breast,
Or is it one of those taunting dreams that come to
   rob me of my rest?
No—no! thank God, 'tis a dream come true! I
   know he has saved my boy
And the poor old heart that he had lived on hope
   is broken at last by joy!

            —*Lucy M. Blinn.*

FALLEN BY THE WAY.

Don't be a fool and blub, Jim, its a darned good
   thing for you—
You'll find a mate as can carry, and 'll play the
   music too?
I'm done this time, for a dollar—I can hardly get
   my breath;
There's something as tells me, somehow, " Bill
   Joy, you be took for death."
It's a wessel gone bust, and a big un'; I can hard-
   ly speak for blood;
It's the last day's tramp as 'as done it—the hills
   and the miles o' mud.
There ain't not the sign of a light, Jim, in this
   God-forsaken spot—
Hunt for some warter, pardner, for my lips is
   burnin' hot.

How much ha' we took to-day, Jim? Why not a
   single brown,
And our show was one o' the best once, and we
   rode from town to town:
Now it's dirty and old and battered, and the puppets is wus for wear,
And their arms and their legs is shaky, and their
   backs is reg'lar bare.
I ain't done my share o' the work, mate, since I
   went that queer in the chest,
But I done what I could, old fellow, and you know
   as I did my best;
And now—well, I'm done, I reckon; it's life as is
   flowing fast—
Stick to me, Jim—don't leave me; it's the end as
   is come at last.

There's Toby a waggin his tail there; poor chap,
   how he'll miss me, Jim!—
Whoever you takes for mate, mind, they ain't to
   be 'ard on 'im;
For I 'ad him a six weeks' puppy, and I taught
   him to box with Punch—
What was that sound in the distance? I fancied
   I heard a scrunch.
Nothin'—ah, well, no matter! I thought 'twas a
   footstep p'r'aps,
A traveler as might ha' helped us, or one o' them
   farmer chaps.
A doctor might stop the bleedin': but there's
   never a chance o' one.
I'll be cold and dead in the mornin'—yer poor old
   pardner's done.

I feel just as if I was chokin' and I'm, oh, so faint
   and low;
Prop me agen the boxes, so I can see the show—
The dear old show and the puppets, Judy and
   Punch and all;
I'd like just to see 'em again, Jim—so prop me
   afore I fall.
Oh, the miles that we've been together, I and the
   puppets and you
And Toby, our faithful Toby—ah, when the show
   was new!
Do ye think of the time, old fellow, when first we
   took the road,
And she was with us, God bless her! and never a
   grief we knowed?

It may be as God'll let her look down from the
   sky to-night,
From out o' the stars up yonder, where she sits in
   the Halls o' Light—
Look down on the poor old showman and see as
   his time is nigh,
And he's comin' to join his darlin' where there's
   never no more Good-bye!
Oh, Jim, how I well remember the night as my
   sweetheart died,
When she lay by the wee dead baby, only a nine-
   months' bride.
'Twas the fall from the stilts as did it, and the
   wild, rough life we led;
D'ye mind what she whispered dyin'—the beautiful words she said?

'Twas when she knew she was goin'; I'm seeing
   her wan white cheek
And the sweet sad smile that lit it when she tried
   so hard to speak;
When she took our hands and joined 'em, and
   bade us, through bad and good,
Be pals, and stick tight to each other! and both
   on us said we would.
I knew as you loved her fust, Jim, and had loved
   her all along,
And I see how you 'id your feelin's when you see
   as you'd counted wrong:
But you stuck like a pal to the show, Jim, and you
   worked and whistled away,
And she never guessed your secret, or she would-
   n't ha' been so gay.

I fancy the dear old days, Jim, when she was
   alive, poor lass—
The feasts that we had by the hedges, and the
   chats in the long green grass,
And the cosy nights at the taverns, when the coin
   came rolling in;
How we laughed when we puffed our baccy, and
   pretended to drink our gin!
Then Toby, a gay young fellow, would lie by the
   fire and doze,
While the missis worked at the puppets and al-
   tered and turned their clo's!

And Judy and Punch and Joey were never so
  smart before,
And the Ghost had a nice white gown on, as a
  clergyman might ha' wore.

She went in the cruel Winter, when the bread
  was hard to get,
When we tramped and slept in the cowshed, hun-
  gry and cold and wet.
How far am I from her grave, Jim ? Ah, a hun-
  dred miles maybe;
To lie by the side o' one's darlin' ain't meant for
  the likes o' me.
The parish 'll bury me here, Jim—here where I
  chance to die;
Come to the grave and see me and bid me a last
  good-bye.
You can bring the show and the puppets, and
  Toby, and beat the drum ;
Who knows but that I may hear it in the wonder-
  ful Kingdom Come ?

I'm goin', old pal—don't blubber and look with
  that skeered white face!
Stand by me here to the last, lad; it's a horrible
  lonely place;
Stoop, for I'll have to whisper—oh, my eyes grow
  strange and dim,
And I feel like poor old Punch feels when the
  hangman comes to him.
I warn't much use as a pardner, and I ain't not
  been for a year,
This bustin' o' wessels and corfin' has made me
  that awful queer,
I'd like to ha' got to a willage or ha' crawled as
  fur as a shed;
Jim, if I lose my senses, stay till yer know I'm
  dead.

Oh, it's hard to die in the open—here on a country
  road;
That's a matter of sentymunt, ain't it ? well sen-
  tymunt jes' be blowed!
For where can a cove die better than under a star-
  lit sky,
With his pardner's arms about him and a tear in
  his pardner's eye ?
Now I want yer to do me a favor—it's the last as
  I'll ask ye, Jim—
There's a mist comin' over my eyeballs, and my
  senses seems to swim;
Set up the show in the road there—there where
  the moonlight be—
Let down the balze and work it, now, while I've
  strength to see.

Give me the drum a minit—I can hardly raise the
  stick ;
Now, are ye ready, pardner ?—up with the curtain,
  quick!
The blood comes faster and faster—that's it! Ah,
  Punch, old boy,
And Judy, and there's the Baby, and Toby, the
  children's joy.
Poor Toby, he knows there's trouble ; for see how
  he hangs his tail;
Bark at the Bobby, Toby, he's a-takin' old Punch
  to jail.
Where have you gone to, pardner ? Where have
  you put the show ?
I see but the big, black shadows that darker and
  darker grow.

I know what it is—the signal! Put down the
  pipes and drum.
I'm off to the distant country—the touch on the
  shoulder's come.
Shall I take any message for you, Jim ! I shall
  see her up there, maybe,
And I'll tell her how hard you worked, pal, and
  the pal as you've been to me,

Jim, when I'm gone I wants yer just to look in
  the box and take
The ragged old dress we kept there and treasured
  for her sweet sake—
The dress that she made for Judy—and lay it upon
  my breast;
And I want you, the day I'm buried, to give the
  show a rest.

Bring 'em away to the churchyard and show 'em
  their master's grave.
Now take up your pipes and blow 'em, and tip us
  a farewell stave.
Mind, when you're choosin' a mate, Jim, don't
  have a rogue or muff;
Make him handle the puppets gentle, for they've
  never been treated rough.
Give me the dog a minit—see how he licks my
  cheek,
Now for a tune on the pipes, mate, and speak as
  the puppets speak ;
It's the music I've lived my life to—let me hear it
  again and die.
I'm a-goin' to her—I'm goin'—God bless yer, Jim!
  —good-bye.

—*Geo. R. Sims.*

DAVY'S PROMISE; OR, I MUST BE THERE ON NEW YEAR'S DAY.

Written by Con. T. Murphy. Recited by John
  Wills of the Novelty Four.

Trudging. along at early dawn on a cold Decem-
  ber morn—
That on which the old year dies and before the
  new is born—
Came a gentle youth, with hair of gold, shivering
  from the bitter cold,
With shoeless feet and box on back, the switchman heard him say—
"I will not give up, for there is the track, and I
  said I'd come on New Year's day."

"All aboard!" The train moves off with its load
  of human freight,
And a moment more and the little lad with box
  would be too late;
But on the platform, with firm hold, stands the
  shivering lad with hair of gold.

"Come, come, my lad, I want my fare."
"I got no money, sir, to pay, and I cannot walk
  no more, and I must be there,
For I said I'd come on New Year's day."

"You must be there! What's that to me ? I have
  heard such tales before ;
I want my fare. It's very cold—come in and shut
  the door.
Where do you wish to go, my lad ? You got no
  money, well, that's too bad !"
"I want to go to Dover's Creek, but that's so very
  far away,
I couldn't walk it in a week, and I must be there
  on New Year's day."

"Sit down, my lad—come closer still; I am sure
  you must be cold.
Blacking boots, is that your trade ? You can't be
  ten years old!
Your name, what might it be ? to Dover ? Whom
  do you go to see ? "
"The bootblacks call me little Dave; I will be
  ten years old in May.
I go to see my mother's grave, and I must be there
  on New Year's day."

"Your mother dead, your father, Davy, where is
   he?"
"Don't ask me, please. Father's dead, but not
   like mother, dead to me,
Seven years ago, so mother said, he done some
   deed for which he fled;
Now mother lies beside the old church where we
   used to play,
And before she died I promised I would always
   come on New Year's day."

"Brave little lad, you shall not break your promise
   with the dead;
Go, visit her, and may God pour choice blessings
   on your head,
And always hold her memory dear; though far
   away, she is ever near
To watch and guard you on your way;
Remember her holy love, and keep your word on
   New Year's day."

"Dover Creek!" the brakeman shouts, in voice
   both loud and clear.
Box on back, off on the track jumps the boy with
   the golden hair
And there he stands with the bitter past, just as
   the old year breathes its last.
And a moment more and he is at the gate of the
   churchyard old and gray.
"Oh, mother dear, I am not too late; I said I'd
   come on New Year's day."

Long years have passed since that cold morn when
   the lad with hair of gold
Came plodding along with box on back, and
   shivering from the cold;
And many a new grave has been made in the
   churchyard where his mother's laid.
Old age has bent his form a-low—he will be
   eighty-five in May;
And at his mother's grave, in rain or snow, he
   asks her blessing on New Year's day.

KATE MALONEY.

In the winter, when the snowdrift stood against
   the cabin door,
Kate Maloney, wife of Patrick, lay nigh dying on
   the floor—
Lay on rags and tattered garments, moaning out
   with feeble breath,
"Knale beside me, Pat, my darlint; pray the
   Lord to give me death."

Patrick knelt him down beside her, took her thin
   and wasted hand,
Saying something to her softly that she scarce
   could understand,
"Let me save ye, oh, my honey! Only spake a
   single word,
And I'll sell the golden secret where it's wanted
   to be heard.

"Sore it cuts my heart to see ye lyin' dyin' day
   by day,
When it's food and warmth ye're wanting just to
   dhrive yer pains away.
There's a hundred golden guineas at my mercy if
   ye will—
*Do ye know that Mickey Regan's in the hut upon
   the hill?"*

Kate Maloney gripped her husband, then she
   looked him through and through
"Pat Maloney, am I dhraming? Did I hear them
   words o' you?
Have I lived an honest woman, loving Ireland,
   God and thee,
That now upon my deathbed ye should spake
   them words to me?

"Come ye here, ye tremblin' traitor; stand beside
   me now, and swear
By yer soul and yer hereafter, while he lives ye
   will not dare
Whisper e'en a single letter o' brave Mickey
   Regan's name.
Can't I die o' cold and hunger? Would ye have
   me die o' shame?

"Let the Saxon bloodhounds hunt him, let them
   show their filthy gold;
What's the poor boy done to hurt 'em? Killed a
   rascal rich and old—
Shot an English thief who robbed us, grinding
   Irish peasants down;
Raisin' rints to pay his wantoms and his lackeys
   up in town.

"We are beasts, we Irish peasants, whom these
   Saxon tyrants spurn;
If ye hunt a beast too closely, and ye wound him
   won't he turn?
Wasn't Regan's sister ruined by the blackguard
   lying dead,
Who was paid his rint last Monday, not in silver,
   but in lead?"

Pat Maloney stood and listened, then he knelt
   and kissed his wife:
"Kiss me, darlint, and forgive me; sure, I thought
   to save your life;
And it's hard to see you dyin' when the gold's
   within my reach.
I'll be lonely when ye're gone, dear—" here a
   whimper stopped his speech.

   *   *   *   *   *   *

Late that night, when Kate was dozing, Pat crept
   cautiously away
From his cabin to the hovel where the hunted
   Regan lay;
He was there—he heard him breathing; some-
   thing whispered to him " Go!
Go and claim the hundred guineas—Kate will
   never need to know."

He would plan some little story when he brought
   her food to eat,
He would say the priest had met him, and had
   sent her wine and meat.
No one passed their lonely cabin; Kate would lie
   and fancy still
Mick had slipped away in secret from the hut
   upon the hill.

Kate Maloney woke and missed him; guessed
   his errand there and then;
Raised her feeble voice and cursed him with the
   curse of God and men
From her rags she slowly staggered, took her
   husband's loaded gun.
Crying, "God, I pray Thee, help me, ere the
   traitor's deed be done!"

All her limbs were weak with fever as she crawled
   across the floor;
But she writhed and struggled bravely till she
   reached the cabin door,
Thence she scanned the open country, for the
   moon was in its prime,
And she saw her husband running, and she
   thought, "there yet is time."

He had come from Regan's hiding, past the door,
   and now he went
By the pathway down the mountain, on his evil
   errand bent.
Once she called him, but he stopped not, neither
   gave he glance behind.
For her voice was weak and feeble, and it melted
   on the wind.

Then a sudden streng/h came to her, and she rose
and followed fast,
Though her naked limbs were frozen by the bitter
winter blast;
She had reached him very nearly when her new-
born spirit fled,
"God has willed it!" cried the woman, *then she
shot the traitor dead!*

From her bloodless lips, half frozen, rose a
whisper to the sky—
"I have saved his soul from treason; here, O
Heaven, let me die.
Now, no babe unborn shall curse him, nor his
country loathe his name
"I have saved ye, oh, my husband, from a death
of deathless shame."

No one yet has guessed their story. Mickey
Regan got away,.
And across the kind Atlantic lives a honest man
to-day;
While in Galway still the peasants show the lonely
mountain-side
Where an Irishman was murdered and an Irish-
woman died.

—*Dagonet.*

THE SEAMSTRESS'S STORY.

How do I feel to-day, Jane? Why, middlin'; what
else could be
A lone and a lorn grass-widder with a babby upon
her knee,
Just eighteen months and teethin', and cuttin'
'em crossways, too?
Pore lamb! half a loaf in the cupboard, and three
weeks of the room's rent due.

But these are trials I'm used to, and trials as can
be bore,
And I'm promised some work, Jane--greatcoats
from the Army Clothin' Store;
And liberally they pay us, at one-and-eleven a
head,
Out of which, Jane, you finds the needles, and
likewise you buys the thread.

Just a twelvemonth since my Bill left me--a
twelvemonth, or maybe more,
Since the partin' blow he gave me sent me flyin'
across the floor!
Bill was handy-like with his fists, Jane, as every-
one jined to agree,
And he kept hisself up to the mark, Jane--he
practiced so much on me.

I never complained? It's likely! myself to my-
self I kep'—
I was proud-like. Look out on the landin', I fancy
I heard a step,
A step as was once familiar, though I can't say as
it was dear,
Unless when—— Me faint? No; laws bless you!
but it give me a flutterin'--*here*.

I was likely enough as a gal, Jane, as smart a
wench as you'd see,
And I was soft upon Willam, and William was nuts
on me;
And so like a fool I gives warning to missus, and
we was wed,
And, twenty-four hours after, he caught me a
crack on the head.

That was the first. But, bless you! harder one
came, and wuss.
And every blow that he planted, he follered up
with a cuss;
And I grew hard and careless and let the place go
to rack,
And when he "upped" with the shovel, I gave
him the poker back!

So things went on till the kid come, and then they
was quiet a bit.
And Bill he grew somewhat softer to me, and I've
seen him sit
And play with it like--for hours; and often he'd
proudly say,
He'd be able to use his mauleys as well as his dad,
some day.

That wore away in time, Jane, as most things
would do with Bill,
And the old hard times came back, Jane, the old,
old trouble and ill;
And he kep' me shorter than ever for money, and
I was sore
And sick and faint with the hunger,--but still
with the life I bore!

Bore with the gnawing anguish, bore with the
stripes, nor cast
Back again the oaths and curses, as I'd often done
in the past;
But something kept me quiet and brave, and
whatever I did,
Was done for--well you're a mother--you know
'twas for the sake of the kid.

'Till one night he came home a tiger, maddened
and fierce with drink,
And did what, had he been sober, he wouldn't
a-done, I think;
I was used to be beaten, but somehow it made me
wild,
Sent me as mad as Bedlam, when he struck and
abused the child!

I waited until next morning, put my bonnet on,
took the keys,
And went and told my story to a justice of the
peace;
Said my life and child's were in danger, from the
strength of his drunken blows,
And took out a summons against him--how I did
it goodness knows!

But I was mad and blinded, and weary of storm
and strife,
And the dull revengeful cravings of years sprang
into life;
I thought that the law would help me, I knew it
was great and strong,
But I doubted the thing I was doing--I doubted it
all along.

You ought to have seen his face, Jane, you're
one of the laughin' sort,
When the news first came to William that he'd
got to appear in court;
I didn't turn pale or falter, it made my case
stronger when
He glared at me for an instant, and went for me
there and then.

What happened I scarce remember, only the
neighbors found
Me, beaten and bruised and bleeding, down in a
death-like swound
On the floor, when they come back, bringing the
kid from his bit o' play;
For, being prepared for a scuffle, I'd sent him
safe out o' the way.

There's little more to tell you; but when I ap-
        peared in court
More like a dead thing moving than one of the
        livin' sort,
Every thing went agin' him, and they give him
        six months as well
For smashing a few policemen and rioting in his
        cell.

'n he was took away, Jane; but the last words he
        said,
A kind of partin' blessin', keeps ringing still in my
        head:
"You got me lagged, my woman? Ay! you can
        boast, it's true;
But when I come out of prison, damn me, I'll
        swing for you!"

"Swing for me." So he will, Jane, Bill never
        broke his word—
And sure as I live or die, Jane, he'll keep to the
        oath I heard.
Hide? There is no use in hidin'; he'd find me out
        in a trice!
Yes! if the kittle's biling, a cup of tea *would* be
        nice!

And Jemmy shall have some too, Jane, he's down-
        right fond of a sup;
Will he be like his father, my boy, when he's quite
        grown up?
He said he'd swing for me, Jane—how that door
        creaks, my dear!
When he said it he meant to do it . . . Merciful
        God he's here!

*   *   *   *   *   *

Glad? Why, of course I'm glad, Bill, and so is
        Jem, I know,
It's the—joy and—the sudden surprise like that's
        set me a-trembling so;
He's an old friend, you mind, lad, Mrs. Brown,
        from the three-pair back,
We was having a cup together, a cup and a friend-
        ly crack.

Yes, you must go, of course, Jane; you're wanted,
        I know, down-stairs,
And when husband and wife have met, Jane, of
        course they've their private affairs
To talk of; but take the baby, he's regular wild
        and mad
For a game with the kids in the alley—there, tod-
        dle along, my lad!

And Jane—hush! or else he'll hear us—if ever a
        prayer you said,
Say one to-night for a woman in terror and mortal
        dread!
For that look on his face means murder, *He said
        he'd do it and*—See,
He's watching us! Laws! I'm coming. Good-
        night! Kiss the boy for me!

THE MIDNIGHT TRYST.

THE winter wood was gray and chill,
        The moon was old, the winds were dead;
The heart of the wood was wierdly still,
        And she started at her own rustling tread,
As though it were the trail of a shroud;
        And she shuddered as to herself she said:
"If only the owl would cry aloud,
Or the leaf would move that lifts on high
Its dead black finger against the sky;
If these snake-like vines that hang and twine
Would stir or swim in the dim moonshine:
Then I would not faint with this nameless dread."
But the wood was still as the breathless dead;

The leaf did not stir in the gray owl scream.
        And she had come there, fantasy led—
To this weird wild wood—on the faith of a dream,
        When they thought her asleep in her maiden bed.

Three nights, while she slept on her tear-cold
        cheeks,
Her long-lost love in a dream had come,
And said to her low: "The pine will speak
        For me, though the rest of the world is dumb-
The brave old pine in the heart of the wood,
By the still, black pool where last we stood;
At the middle hour of the night go there—
The pine shall a sign and a message bear."

There days she carried the dream close locked
        In her troubled breast, and gave no sign;
They would but mock at the dream as they mocked
        In rage and pride at her face, that could pine
And pale for a faithless lover, long-gone
To a land that the sun shines warm upon.
Gone so long that they could but say,
"He has forsaken her; foul befall
The steps of the traitor, wherever they stray."
        And her bearded brothers, fierce and tall,
Longed with his blood the wrong to pay,
        And chafed when they saw that a dreary pall,
Hung for her on the sunniest day;
        And when a curse on his head they would call,
She would drop her eyes to his ring and pray.
They would have wrenched the ring away,
But that her finger grew so small,
They said, "Of itself it soon must fall."

*   *   *   *   *   *

She has reached the heart of the winter wood—
Stiller and deeper the shadows brood;
She see's the deep pool's glimmering disk,
Where falls one ray from the waning moon;
The pine-tree stands like an obelisk,
        Still, as if carved of the granite stone·
In its dark-plumed top there is no stir—
        Never a breath, nor a voice, nor a moan—
It holds no token no message for her.

She waits, she listens, her hands grow numb,
Close-pressed to her heart to hush its beats;
No sign her straining senses greets
On earth or in air—the pine is dumb;
Yet, as if breathed from a viewless shrine,
Thrills the wordless whisper, "It will come!"
        And breathless she stands and awaits the sign.

What was it? There is no breeze to shake
        The long, light leaf that lifts on high
        Its dead, black finger against the sky;
Yet the pine-boughs suddenly thrill and quake,
        As though a breath of storm swept by—
The pine, that had seemed a shaft of stone
In the stirless wood, it moves alone.
And now a sound, a sigh, a moan—
Wind-like, yet human in its tone—
Fills the low swaying boughs o'erhead,
Lades the air with a spell of dread:
"Dead!" it syllables; "dead—dead—dead!"

Nearer it steals like the wave of the seas.
Her heart is hushed—she sinks to her knees—
Her eyes are closed—she nothing sees;
But a touch that is not the touch of the breeze
Moves through her loosened tresses now—
Falls like a kiss on her wasted brow—
For a sense of perfect peace and love
Bears her up like the wings of a dove.

A moment only, and it is gone!
In the silent wood she stands alone:
The pine does not stir, nor the dead leaf shake,
And the long black shadows sleep on the lake;
A moon-ray falls like an elfin wand—
On the withered lily of her hand—
Glints on the bright bethrothal band.
She kissed the ring. "You are mine," she said;
"I will wear you now till my life is sped!
He is not false—he is only dead!"
                        —*Mary E. Bryan.*

CHRISTMAS DAY IN THE WORKHOUSE.

IT is Christmas day in the workhouse,
  And the cold bare walls are bright
With garlands of green and holly,
  And the place is a pleasant sight:
For with clean-washed hands and faces,
  In a long and hungry line
The paupers sit at the tables,
  For this is the hour they dine.

And the guardians and their ladies,
  Although the wind is east,
Have come in their furs and wrappers
  To watch their charges feast;
To smile and be condescending,
  Put pudding on pauper plates,
To be hosts at the workhouse banquet
  They've paid for—with the rates.

Oh, the paupers are meek and lowly
  With their "Thank'ee kindly, mum's;"
So long as they fill their stomachs,
  What matter whence it comes?
But one of the old men mutters,
  And pushes his plate aside:
"Great God!" he cries; "but it chokes me;
  For this is the day *she* died."

The guardians gazed in horror,
  The master's face went white:
"Did a pauper refuse their pudding?"
  "Could their ears believe aright?"
Then the ladies clutched their husbands
  Thinking the man would die,
Struck by a bolt, or something,
  By the outraged one on high.

But the pauper sat for a moment,
  Then rose 'mid a silence grim,
For the others had ceased to chatter,
  And trembled in every limb.
He looked at the guardian's ladies,
  Then, eyeing their lords, he said:
"I eat not the food of villains
  Whose hands are foul and red,

"Whose victims cry for vengeance
  From their dark, unhallowed graves."
"He's drunk!" said the workhouse master,
  "Or else he's mad, and raves."
"Not drunk or mad," cried the pauper,
  "But only a hunted beast,
Who, torn by the hounds and mangled,
  Declines the vulture's feast.

"I care not a curse for the guardians,
  And I won't be dragged away.
Just let me have the fit out,
  It's only on Christmas day
That the black past comes to goad me,
  And prey on my burning brain,
I'll tell you the rest in a whisper,—
  I swear I won't shout again.

"Keep your hands off me, curse you!
  Hear me right out to the end.
You come here to see how paupers
  The season of Christmas spend,
You come here to watch us feeding,
  As they watch the captured beast,
Hear why a penniless pauper
  Spits on your paltry feast.

Do you think I will take your bounty,
  And let you smile and think
You're doing a noble action
  With the parish's meat and drink?

Where is my wife, you traitors—
  The poor old wife you slew?
Yes, by the God above us,
  My Nance was killed by you!

"Last winter my wife lay dying,
  Starved in a filthy den;
I had never been to the parish,—
  I came to the parish then.
I swallowed my pride in coming,
  For, ere the ruin came,
I held up my head as a trader,
  And I bore a spotless name,

"I came to the parish, craving
  Bread for a starving wife,
Bread for the woman who'd loved me
  Through fifty years of life;
And what do you think they told me,
  Mocking my awful grief?
That 'the House' was open to us,
  But they wouldn't give 'out relief.'

"I slunk to the filthy alley—
  'Twas a cold, raw Christmas eve—
And the bakers' shops were open,
  Tempting a man to thieve:
But I clenched my fists together,
  Holding my head awry,
So I came to her empty-handed
  And mournfully told her why.

"Then I told her 'the House' was open;
  She had heard of the ways of *that*,
For her bloodless cheeks went crimson,
  And up in her rags she sat,
Crying, 'Bide the Christmas here, John,
  We've never had one apart;
I think I can bear the hunger,—
  The other would break my heart.'

"All through that eve I watched her,
  Holding her hand in mine,
Praying the Lord, and weeping
  Till my lips were salt as brine.
I asked her once if she hungered,
  And as she answered 'No,'
The moon shone in at the window
  Set in a wreath of snow.

"Then the room was bathed in glory,
  And I saw in my darling's eyes
The far-away look of wonder
  That comes when the spirit flies;
And her lips were parched and parted,
  And her reason came and went,
For she raved of our home in Devon,
  Where our happiest years were spent.

"And the accents, long forgotten,
  Came back to the tongue once more,
For she talked like the country lassie
  I woo'd by the Devon shore.
Then she rose to her feet and trembled,
  And fell on the rags and moaned,
And, 'Give me a crust—I'm famished—
  For the love of God!' she groaned.

"I rushed from the room like a madman,
  And flew to the workhouse gate,
Crying 'Food for a dying woman?'
  And the answer came, 'Too late.'
They drove me away with curses;
  Then I fought with a dog in the street,
And tore from the mongrel's clutches
  A crust he was trying to eat.

"Back, through the filthy by-lanes!
  Back, through the trampled slush!
Up to the crazy garret,
  Wrapped in an awful hush.

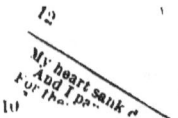

There's little vased down at the threshold,
pearl there in the silvry moonlight
My Nance lay, cold and still.

"Up to the blackened ceiling
The sunken eyes were cast—
I knew on these lips all bloodless
My name ... had been the last:
She'd called for her absent husband—
O God! had I but known!—
Had died in that den—*alone*.
A kind of called in vain, and in anguish
"You ... head

R. "Yes, there, in a land of plenty,
Lay a loving looking woman dead,
Cruelly starved and murdered
For a loaf of the parish bread.
At yonder gate, last Christmas,
I craved for a human life.
You, who would feast us paupers,
What of my murdered wife!

* * * * * *

"There, get ye gone to your dinners;
Don't mind me in the least;
Think of the happy paupers
Eating your Christmas feast;
And when you recount their blessings
In your snug parochial way,
Say what you did for *me*, too,
Only last Christmas Day.
George R. Sims.

THE WOMEN OF MUMBLES HEAD.

BRING, novelist, your note-book! bring, dramatist,
    your pen!
And I'll tell you a simple story of what women do
    for men.
It's only a tale of a life-boat, of the dying and the
    dead—
Of the terrible storm and shipwreck that hap-
    pened off Mumbles Head.
Maybe you have traveled in Wales, sir, and know
    it north and south;
Maybe you are friends with "the natives" that
    dwell at Oystermouth;
It happens, no doubt, that from Bristol you've
    crossed in a casual way,
And have sailed your yacht in the summer in the
    blues of Swansea Bay.

Well, it isn't like that in the winter, when the
    light-house stands alone,
In the teeth of Atlantic breakers that foam on its
    face of stone;
It wasn't like that when the hurricane blew, and
    the storm-bell tolled, or when
There was news of a wreck and the life-boat
    launched, and a desperate cry for men.
When in the world did the coxswain shirk? A
    brave old salt was he!
Proud to the bone of as four strong lads as ever
    had tasted the sea,
Welshmen all to the lungs and loins, who, about
    that coast 'twas said,
Had saved some hundred lives apiece—at a shill-
    ing or so a head!

So, the father launched the life-boat, in the teeth
    of the tempest's roar,
And he stood like a man at the rudder, with an
    eye on his boys at the oar.

Out to the wreck went the father, out to the
    wreck went the sons,
Leaving the weeping of women, and booming of
    signal guns;
Leaving the mother who loved them, and the girls
    that the sailors love,
Going to death for duty, and trusting to God
    above!
Do you murmur a prayer, my brothers, when cozy
    and safe in bed,
For men like these who are ready to die for a
    wreck off Mumbles Head?

It didn't go well with the life-boat; 'twas a ter-
    rible storm that blew!
And it snapped the rope in a second that was
    flung to the drowning crew;
And then the anchor parted—'twas a tussle to
    keep afloat!
But the father stuck to the rudder, and the boys
    to the brave old boat,
Then at last on the poor doomed life-boat a wave
    broke mountains high;
"God help us now!" said the father. "It's over,
    my lads! Good-bye!"
Half of the crew swam shoreward, half to the
    sheltered caves,
But father and sons were fighting death in the
    foam of the angry waves.

Up at a lighthouse window two women beheld the
    storm,
And saw in the boiling breakers a figure—a fight-
    ing form;
It might be a gray-haired father; then the women
    held their breath;
It might be a fair-haired brother, who was having
    a round with death;
It might be a lover, a husband, whose kisses were
    on the lips
Of the women whose love is the life of men going
    down to the sea in ships.
They had seen the launch of the life-boat, they
    had seen the worst, and more,
Then, kissing each other, these women went down
    from the lighthouse straight to shore.

There by the rocks on the breakers these sisters,
    hand in hand,
Beheld once more that desperate man who
    struggled to reach the land.
'Twas only aid he wanted to help him across the
    wave,
But what are a couple of women with only a man
    to save?
What are a couple of women? Well, more than
    three craven men
Who stood by the shore with chattering teeth, re-
    fusing to stir—and then
Off went the women's shawls, sir; in a second
    they're torn and rent,
Then, knotting them into a rope of love, straight
    into the sea they went!

"Come back!" cried the lighthouse keeper, "for
    God's sake, girls, come back!"
As they caught the waves on their foreheads, re-
    sisting the fierce attack.
"Come back!" moaned the gray-haired mother,
    as she stood by the angry sea,
"If the waves take you, my darlings, there's no-
    body left to me!"
"Come back!" said the three strong soldiers, who
    still stood faint and pale,
"You will drown if you face the breakers, you
    will fall if you brave the gale!"
"Come back?" said the girls. "We will not! Go
    tell it to all the town!
We'll lose our lives, God willing, before that man
    shall drown!"

"Give one more knot to the shawls, Bess, give one
  strong clutch of your hand!
Just follow me, brave, to the shingle, and we'll
  bring him safe to land!
Wait for the next wave, darling, only a moment
  more,
And I'll have him safe in my arms, dear, and we'll
  drag him to the shore."
Up to the arms in the water, fighting it breast to
  breast,
They caught and saved a brother alive. God
  bless them! You know the rest.
Well, many a heart beat stronger, and many a
  tear was shed,
And many a glass was tossed right off to "The
  Women of Numbles Head!"

A CHRISTMAS STORY.

PART I.

Up, Gregory! the cloudy east
  Is bright with the break o' the day;
'Tis time to yoke our cattle, and time
  To eat our crust and away.
Up, out o' your bed! for the rosy red
  Will soon be growing gray.

Ay, straight to your feet, my lazy lad,
  And button your jacket on;
Already neighbor Joe is afield
  And so is our neighbor John.
The golden light is turning to white,
  And 'tis time that we were gone.

Nay, leave your shoes hung high and dry—
  Do you fear a little sleet?
Your mother to-day is not by half
  So dainty with her feet;
And I'll warrant you she hadn't a shoe
  At your age to her feet.

What! shiv'ring on an April day?
  Why this is pretty news!
The frosts before an hour will all
  Be melted into dews,
And Christmas week will do, I think,
  To talk about your shoes.

Waiting to brew another cup
  Of porridge? sure you're mad!
One cup at your age, Gregory,
  And precious small, I had.
We cannot bake the Christmas cake
  At such a rate, my lad.

Out, out at once! and on with the yoke!
  Your feet will never freeze!
The sun before we have done a stroke
  Will be in the tops o' the trees.
On Christmas day you may eat and play
  As much as ever you please.

So out of the house and into the sleet,
  With his jacket open wide,
Went pale and patient Gregory—
  All present joy denied—
And yoked his team like one in a dream,
  Hungry and sleepy-eyed.

PART II.

It seemed to our little harvester
  He could hear the shadows creep
For the scythe lay idle in the grass,
  And the reaper had ceased to reap.
'Twas the burning noon of the leafy June,
  And the birds were all asleep.

And he seemed to rather see than hear
  The wind through the long leaves draw,
As he sat and notched the stops along
  His pipe of hollow straw
On Christmas day he had planned to play
  His tune without a flaw.

Upon his sleeve the spider's web
  Hung loose like points of lace;
And he looked like a picture painted there,
  He was so full of grace,
For his cheeks they shone as if there had blown
  Fresh roses in his face

Ah, never on his lady's arm
  A lover's hand was laid
With touches soft as his upon
  The flute that he had made,
As he bent his ear and watched to hear
  The sweet, low tune he played.

But all at once from out his cheek
  The light o' the roses fled—
He had heard a coming step that crushed
  The daisies 'neath its tread.
O, happiness! thou art held by less
  Than the spider's tiniest thread!

A moment, and the old, harsh call
  Had broken his silver tune,
And with his sickle all as bright
  And bent as the early moon,
He cut his way through the thick-set hay
  In the burning heat o' June.

As one who by a river stands,
  Weary and worn and sad,
And sees the flowers the other side
  So was it with the lad.
There was Christmas light in his dream at night,
  But a dream was all he had.

Work, work, in the light o' th' rosy morns,
  Work, work, in the dusky eves;
For now they must plow and now they must plant,
  And now they must bind the sheaves.
And far away was the holiday
  All under the Christmas leaves.

For still it brought the same old cry,
  If he would rest or play,
Some other week, or month, or year,
  But not now—not to-day!
Nor feast nor flower, for th' passing hour,
  But all for the far away.

PART III.

And Christmas came, and Gregory
  With the dawn was broad awake;
But there was the crumple cow to milk,
  And there was the cheese to make;
And so it was noon ere he went to the town
  To buy the Christmas cake.

"You'll leave your warm, new coat at home,
  And keep it fresh and bright
To wear," the careful old man said,
  "When you come back to-night."
"Ay," answered the lad, for his heart was glad,
  And he whistled out of their sight.

The frugal couple sat by the fire
  And talked the hours away.
Turning over the years like leaves
  To the friends of their wedding day—
Saying who was wed and who was dead,
  And who was growing gray.

And so at last the day went by,
  As, somehow, all days will;
And when the evening winds began
  To blow up wild and shrill.
They looked to see if their Gregory
  Were coming across the hill.

They saw the snow-cloud on the sky,
  With its rough and ragged edge,
And thought of the river running high,
  And thought of the broken bridge;
But they did not see their Gregory
  Keeping his morning's pledge!

The old wife rose, her fear to hide,
  And set the house aright;
But oft she paused at the window side,
  And looked out on the night.
The candles fine, they were all ashine,
  But they could not make it light.

The very clock ticked mournfully,
  And the cricket was not glad ;
And to the old folks sitting alone
  The time was, oh, so sad!
For the Christmas light, it lacked that night
  The cheeks of their little lad.

The winds and the woods fall wrestling now,
  And they cry as the storm draws near,
" If Gregory were but home alive,
  He should not work all this year! "
For they saw him dead in the river's bed,
  Through the surges of their fear.

Of ghosts that walk o' nights they tell—
  A sorry Christmas theme—
And of signs and tokens in the air,
  And of many a warning dream,
Till the bough at the pane through th' sleet and
    rain
  Drags like a corpse in a stream.

There was the warm new coat unworn,
  And the flute of straw unplayed;
And these were dreadfuler than ghosts
  To make their souls afraid.
As the years that were gone came one by one,
  And their slights before them laid.

The Easter days and the Christmas days
  Bereft of their sweet employ,
And working and waiting through them all
  Their little pale-eyed boy,
Looking away to the holiday
  That should bring the promised joy.

" God's mercy on us! " cried they both,
  " We have been so blind and deaf;
And justly are our gray heads bowed
  To the very grave with grief!"
But hark! is't th' rain that taps at th' pane,
  Or the fluttering, falling leaf?

Nay, fluttering leaf, nor snow, nor rain,
  However hard they strive,
Can make a sound so sweet and soft,
  Like a bee's wing in the hive.
Joy! joy! O joy! it is their boy!
  Safe, home, in their arms alive!

Ah, never was their pair so rich
  As they that night, I trow;
And never a lad in all the world
  With a merrier pipe to blow,
Nor Christmas light that shone so bright
  At midnight on the snow.
                              —Alice Carey.

THE LAST HYMN.

The Sabbath day was ending in a village by the
    sea;
The uttered benediction touch the people tenderly,
And they rose to face the sunset in the glowing,
    lighted West,
And then hastened to their dwellings for God's
    blessed boon of rest.

But they looked across the waters, and a storm
    was raging there;
A fierce spirit moved above them—the wild spirit
    of the air—
And it lashed and shook and tore them, till they
    thundered, groaned and boomed;
And alas for any vessel in their yawning gulfs
    entombed.

Very anxious were the people on that rocky coast
    of Wales,
Lest the dawn of coming morrow should be telling
    awful tales.
When the sea had spent its passion and should
    cast upon the shore
Bits of wreck and swollen victims, as it had done
    heretofore.

With the rough winds blowing round her, a brave
    woman strained her eyes,
And she saw along the billows a large vessel fall
    and rise.
Oh! it did not need a prophet to tell what the end
    must be,
For no ship could ride in safety near that shore on
    such a sea.

Then the pitying people hurried from their homes
    and thronged the beach.
Oh! for power to cross the waters and the perish-
    ing to reach!
Helpless hands were wrung for sorrow, tender
    hearts were cold with dread,
And the ship, urged by the tempest, to the fatal
    rock-shore sped.

"She has parted in the middle! Oh! the half of
    her goes down!
God have mercy! Is Heaven far to seek for those
    who drown?"
Lo! when next the white, shocked faces looked
    with terror on the sea.
Only one last clinging figure on the spar was seen
    to be.

Nearer the trembling watchers came the wreck
    tossed by the wave,
And the man still clung and floated, though no
    power on earth could save.
"Could we send him a short message? Here's a
    trumpet shout away!"
'Twas the preacher's hand that took it, and he
    wondered what to say.

Any memory of his sermon? Firstly? Secondly?
    Ah, no!
There was but one thing to utter in the awful hour
    of woe;
So he shouted through the trumpet: "Look to
    Jesus! Can you hear?"
And "Ay, ay, sir!" rang the answer, o'er the
    waters, loud and clear.

Then they listened. "He is singing 'Jesus, Lover
    of my soul,'"
And the winds brought back the echo, "While the
    nearer waters roll."
Strange, indeed, it seemed to hear him, "Till the
    storm of life is past."
Singing bravely from the waters, "Oh, receive my
    soul at last!"

He could have no other refuge, "Hangs my helpless soul on Thee
Leave, ah, leave me not—" The singer dropped
  at last into the sea.
And the watchers, looking homeward through
  their eyes with tears made dim,
Said, "He passed to be with Jesus in the singing
  of that hymn."
  —*Marianne Farningham.*

'OSTLER JOE.

I STOOD at eve when the sun went down,
  By a grave where a woman lies,
Who lured men's souls to the shores of sin
  With the light of her wanton eyes;
Who sang the song that the siren sang
  On the treacherous Lurley height;
Whose face was fair as a summer's day,
  And whose heart was as black as night.

Yet a blossom I fain would pluck to-day
  From the garden above her dust—
Not the languorous lily of soulless sin,
  Nor the blood-red rose of lust—
But a sweet white blossoms of holy love
  That grew in that one green spot
In the arid desert of Phrynes' life
  Where all else was parched and hot.

In the summer, when the meadows
  Were aglow with blue and red,
Joe, the 'ostler of "The Magpie,"
  And fair Annie Smith were wed
Plump was Annie, plump and pretty,
  With a face as fair as snow;
He was anything but handsome,
  Was the "Magpie's" 'ostler, Joe.

But he won the winsome lassie;
  They'd a cottage and a cow—
And her matronhood sat lightly,
  On the village beauty's brow;
Sped the months, and came a baby—
  Such a blue-eyed baby boy!
Joe was working in the stables
  When they told him of his joy—

He was rubbing down the horses—
  Gave them, then and there,
All a special feed of clover,
  Just in honor of his heir.
It had been his great ambition
  (And he told the horses so)
That the fates would send a baby
  Who might bear the name of *Joe.*

Little Joe, the child was christened,
  And like babies grew apace.
He'd his mother's eyes of azure,
  And his father's honest face.
Swift the happy years went over,
  Years of blue and cloudless sky;
Love was lord of that small cottage
  And the tempest passed them by.

Down the lane by Annie's cottage
  Chanced a gentleman to roam;
He caught a glimpse of Annie
  In her bright and happy home.
Thrice he came and saw her sitting
  By the window with her child;
And he nodded to the baby,
  And the baby laughed and smiled.

So at last it grew to know him
  (Little Joe was nearly four)
He would call the pretty "gemplum"
  As he passed the open door;

And one day he ran and caught him
  And in child's play pulled him in;
And the baby Joe had prayed for,
  Brought about the mother's sin.

'Twas the same old wretched story,
  That for ages bards have sung;
'Twas a woman, weak and wanton,
  And a villain's tempting tongue;
'Twas a picture deftly painted
  For a silly creature's eyes,
Of the Babylonian wonders
  And the joy that in them lies.

Annie listened and was tempted—
  Was tempted and she fell,
As the angels fell from Heaven
  To the lowest depths of hell.
She was promised wealth and splendor
  And a life of genteel sloth;
Yellow gold, for child and husband—
  And the woman left them both.

Home, one eve, came Joe, the 'ostler,
  With a cheery cry of "*Wife?*"
Finding that which blurred forever
  All the story of his life.
She had left a silly letter;
  Through the cruel scrawl he spelt,
Then he sought the lonely bedroom,
  Joined his horny hands and knelt.

"Now, O Lord, O God, forgive her,
  For she ain't to blame," he cried;
"For I ought to seen her trouble
  And 'a gone away and died.
Why, a girl like her—God bless her—
  'Twasn't likely as her'd rest
With her bonny head *forever*
  On a 'ostler's ragged breast.

"It was kind 'o her to bear with me
  All the long and happy time;
So for my sake please to bless her,
  Though you count her deed a crime.
If so be I don't pray proper,
  Lord, forgive me, for you see
I can talk all right to 'osses,
  But I'm kind o' strange with Thee."

Ne'er a line came to the cottage,
  From the woman who had flown;
Joe, the baby, died that winter,
  And the man was left alone.
Ne'er a bitter word he uttered,
  But in silence kissed the rod,
Saving what he told his horses,
  Saving what he told his God.

Far away in mighty London
  Rose the wanton into fame,
For her beauty won men's homage,
  And she prospered in her shame.
Quick from lord to lord she flitted,
  Higher still each prize she won;
And her rivals paled beside her
  As the stars beside the sun.

Next she trod the stage half naked,
  And she dragged a temple down
To the level of a market
  For the women of the town.
And the kisses she had given
  To poor 'ostler Joe for naught,
With their gold and priceless jewels
  Rich and titled roues bought.

Went the years with flying footsteps
  While her star was at its height;
Then the darkness came on swiftly,
  And the gloaming turned to-night.

shattered strength and faded beauty
Tore the laurels from her brow;
Of the thousands who had worshipped
Never one came near her now.

Broken down in health and fortune,
Men forgot her very name;
Till the news that she was dying
Woke the echoes of her fame.
And the papers in their gossip,
Mentioned how an actress lay
Sick to death in humble lodgings,
Growing weaker every day.

One there was who read the story
In a far-off country place;
And that night the dying woman
Woke and looked upon his face.
Once again the strong arms clasped her
That had clasped her long ago;
And her weary head lay pillowed
Upon the breast of 'ostler Joe.

All the past he had forgiven—
All the sorrow and the shame;
He had found her sick and lonely,
And his wife he now could claim.
Since the grand folks who had known her
One and all had slunk away,
He could clasp his long lost darling,
And no man could say him nay.

In his arms death found her lying,
From his arms her spirit fled;
And his tears came down in torrents
As he knelt beside his dead.
Never once his love had faltered
Through her sad, unhallowed life,
And the stone above her ashes
Bears the sacred name of *wife*.

That's the blossom I fain would pluck to-day
From the garden above her dust;
Not the languorous lily of soulless sin,
Nor the blood-red rose of lust;
But a sweet white blossom of holy love,
That grew in the one green spot
In the arid desert of Phryne's life,
Where all else was parched and hot.
                        —*George R. Sims.*

THE TRAMP'S STORY.

If experience has gold in it (as discerning folks
    agree),
Then there's quite a little fortune stowed away
    somewhere in me,
And I deal it out regardless of a regular stated
    price,
In rough-done-up prize packages of common-
    sense advice;
The people they can take it or run round it, as
    they please,
But the best thing they'll find in it is some
    words like unto these:
*Worm or beetle, drought or tempest, on a farmer's
    land may fall,*
*But for first-class ruination, trust a mortgage
    'gainst them all.*

On my weddin' day my father touched me kindly
    on the arm,
And handed me the papers for an eighty-acre
    farm,
With the stock an' tools an' buildin's for an inde-
    pendent start,
Saying, "Here's a weddin' present from my
    muscle and my heart;

And, except the admonitions you have taken
    from my tongue,
And the reasonable lickens that you had when
    you was young,
And your food and clothes and schoolin' (not as
    much as I could wish,
For I had a number eatin' from a some'at scanty
    dish),
And the honest love you captured when you first
    sat on my knee,
This is all I have to give you—so expect no more
    from me."

People'd said I couldn't marry the sweet girl I
    tried to court,
Till we smiling submitted a minority report;
Then they laid their theories over, with a quick-
    ness queer to see.
And said they knew we'd marry, but we never
    could agree;
But we did not frame and hang up all the neigh-
    bors had to say,
But ran out little heaven in our own peculiar way;
We started off quite jolly, wondrous full of health
    and cheer,
And a general understanding that the road was
    pretty clear.

So we lived and toiled and prospered; and the lit-
    tle family party
That came on from heaven to visit us were bright
    and hale and hearty;
And to-day we might ha' been there had I only
    just have known
How to lay my road down solid, and let well
    enough alone.
But I soon commenced a-kicking in the traces, I
    confess,
There was too much land that joined me that I
    didn't yet possess.
When once he gets land-hungry, strange how
    ravenous one can be!
'Twasn't long before I wanted all the ground
    that I could see.
So I bought another eighty (not foreboding any
    harm),
And for that and some down-money, put a mort-
    gage on my farm.
Then I brought another forty, hired some cash
    to fix up new,
And to buy a covered carriage—and of course the
    mortgage grew.
Now my wife was square against this, 'tis but
    right that you should know,
(Though I'm very far from saying that I think it's
    always so);
But she went in hearty with me, working hard
    from day to day,
For we knew that life was business, now we had
    that debt to pay.

We worked through Spring and Winter, through
    Summer and through Fall,
But that mortgage worked the hardest and the
    steadiest of us all;
It worked on nights and Sundays; it worked
    each holiday;
It settled down among us, and it never went
    away.
Whatever we kept from it seemed a'most as bad
    as theft;
It watched us every minute, and it ruled us right
    and left.
The rust and blight were with us sometimes, and
    sometimes they were not;
The dark-browed, scowling mortgage was ever
    on the spot.
The weevil and the cut-worm they went as well as
    came;
The mortgage stayed forever, eating hearty all
    the same.

It nailed up every window, stood guard at every
  door,
And happiness and sunshine made their home
  with us no more;
Till with failing crops and sickness we got stalled
  upon the grade,
And there came a dark day on us, when the in-
  terest wasn't paid;
And there came a sharp foreclosure, and I kind
  o' lost my head,
And grew weary and discouraged, and the farm
  was sold and fled.
The children left and scattered when they hardly
  yet were grown;
My wife she pined and perished, an' I found my-
  self alone.
What she died of was "a mystery," and the doc-
  tors never knew;
But *I* knew she died of *mortgage*—just as well's
  I wanted to.
If to trace a hidden sorrow were within the doc-
  tor's art,
They'd ha' found a mortgage lying on that wom-
  an's broken heart.

Two different kinds of people the devil most as-
  sails;
One is the man who conquers; the other, he who
  fails.
But still I think the last kind are soonest to give
  up.
And to hide their sorry faces behind the shame-
  ful cup;
Like some old king or other, whose name I've
  somehow lost,
The straightway tear their eyes out, just when
  they need 'em most,
When once I had discovered that the debt I could
  not pay,
I tried to liquidate it in a rather common way;
I used to meet in private a fellow-financier,
And we would drink ourselves worth ten thou-
  sand dollars clear—
As easy a way to prosper as ever has been found,
But one's a heap sight poorer when he gets back
  to the ground.

Of course I ought to ha' braced up, an' worked on
  all the same;
I ain't a-trying to shirk out, or cover up from
  blame;
But still I think men often, it safely may be said,
Are *driven* to temptations, in place of being led;
And if that tyrant mortgage hadn't cracked its
  whip at me,
I shouldn't have constituted the ruin that you see.
For though I've never stolen or defaulted, please
  to know
Yet, socially considered, I am pretty middlin'
  low.
I am helpless and forsaken: I am childless and
  alone;
I haven't a single dollar that it's fair to call my
  own;
My old age knows no comfort, my heart is scant
  o'cheer;
The children they run from me as soon as I come
  near;
The women shrink and tremble—their alms are
  fear-bestowed;
The dogs howl curses at me, and hunt me down
  the road.
My home is where night finds me; my friends
  are few and cold;
Oh, little is there in this world for one who's
  poor and old!
But I'm wealthy in experience, all put up in good
  advice,
To take or not to take it, with no difference in
  the price;

You may have it, an' thrive on it, or run round it,
  as you please,
But I generally give it wrapped up in such words
  as these;
*Worm or beetle, drought or tempest, on a farmer's
  land may fall,
But for first-class ruination, trust a mortgage
  'gainst them all.*
                              —*Will Carleton.*

THE MOONSHINER'S DAUGHTER.

THE men was away at the wild-cat still,
  When one of them artist chaps
Stopped at the cabin of Moonshiner Bill
  And dropped on the porch his traps.
He asked for a drink of water—
  It being a warmish day—
And when little Katie brought it,
  He asked her to let him stay,
And rest on the shady porch awhile,
  And Katie, who never spoke til
Said "yes," with a smile, and never a thought
  Of the hid-away mountain still.

Presently Moonshiner Bill came home,
  And his gal waitin' down by the gate,
Cried, "Dad, there's a nice-talkin' stranger
  come;
Now, a kiss, please, for little Kate."
The artist riz to his feet and said:
  "I'm sorry to so intrude;
But love of nature my steps have led
  To this picturesque solitude."
Talk so pert and proper and fine
  Sorter stunted old Bill,
And he dropped a jug of new moonshine
  He had packed from the wild-cat still.

The artist spy staid day after day,
  Sketchin' and actin' his part,
And when he left to go on his way
  He carried off little Kate's heart.
She watched for his comin' soon and late,
  As she turned her wheel and spun,
And the gray owl hooted, "Who is true?"
  And the frogs said, "Nary one."
But he came at last one set of sun,
  As she watched the road to the glen,
She saw him ride in his uniform
  At the head of the government men.

She thought that his solemnly plighted vows,
  He had made to break at will,
And with flashin' eyes she left the house
  To signal the men at the still.
She ran like a deer; but the cavalrymen
  Charged the still at a rattlin' gait,
And when she reached the head of the glen
  She knew she had come too late;
For some were captured, but Bill wer game,
  He stood his ground on the hill
'Till they pressed him close, then when he run
  'Twas cussin' and fightin' still.

"After him, men!" the captain cried,
  And he dashed down the ravine's bed;
"We'll prove his boastin' threat is a lie—
  We'll take him alive or dead."
At this Bill halted, cocked his gun,
  Drawed a sure bead, bound to shoot
The man a comin' down that ravine
  In deadly and close pursuit.
That man never seed his bush-hid foe
  Till Kate leaped down the rock,
And sprung to meet that leaden death,
  Her heart stopped the bullet's shock.

She reeled and fell, and the man whose life
 She saved at the cost of her own,
Cried, "God of heaven! My darling Kate!"
 And dropped on his knees with a groan.
From the rocky ground he raised her head;
 Her blue eyes shone with bliss.
She smiled on him as she faintly said:
 "I'm dyin'—for you—one kiss."
Then the lovin' light that filled her eyes
 Grew dim, and the angel Peace
Stooped from the shinin' world beyond,
 And gave her spirit release.
        —M. B.

THE BABY'S PRAYER.

'Twas evening, and the baby
 Knelt down beside my knee,
To say in lisping accents
 Her prayers after me.
Her dimpled hands were folded;
 Her golden head was bent;
With grace and sweet devotion
 Her attitude was blent.
She repeated, "Our Papa,"
 Which in the heavens art,
While every word she uttered
 Found echo in my heart.

Then came, "And now I lay me
 Down in my bed to seep;
I pay the Lord, dear mama,
 My ittle soul to teep!
And Dod bess ou and papa,
 Ganpa and gamma, too,
Aunties and little cuddens,
 And all my fenz"—not few.
And then her sweet petitions
 Rose earnestly and clear,
And she prayed for "Unker Eddie
 And all poor solzers dear."

Before amen was uttered
 The baby raised her head,
With thought born sure of heaven,
 "And the mebels, too?" she said.
"Yes darling." (For the rebels,
 I thought, could not despise
Her innocent, sweet petitions
 Ascending to the skies.)
Again, with eyes uplifted—
 Those eyes of heavenly blue—
She lisped with reverent accent,
 "Lord, bess the mebels, too."

And so through all the horror
 Of that fratricidal war,
Whose cruel tide was rolling
 O'er the southern lands afar,
Baby ne'er forgot her "mebels,"
 Though prompted not by me,
At morn or eve, when bending
 In prayer beside my knee.
Ah! 'tis from lips like baby's—
 That little sinless child—
God perfects praise forever,
 True, sweet and undefiled.

How often I had wondered
 What the "mebels" would have said,
Had they known, in Massachusetts
 A babe with golden head
Was over and over lisping
 A prayer in Jesus's name,
That the north and south together
 His blessing soon might claim.
The mothers, I knew, would love her—
 My baby free from sin—
For a touch of baby nature
 Will make all mothers kin.

So when the war was over
 And peace again had smiled,
I told two southern warriors
 Of the prayers of the child,
Who had grown a little taller,
 But not one bit less sweet,
Than when she craved a blessing
 For the "mebels" at my feet—
They said, as they kissed the darling
 Again and yet again,
With lifted face and streaming eyes,
 "God bless the child, Amen!"
     —Mrs. E. E. Williamson.

THE ENGINE DRIVER'S STORY.

We were driving the down express—
 Will at the steam, I at the coal—
Over the valleys and villages!
Over the marshes and coppices!
Over the river deep and broad!
Through the mountain, under the road!
Flying along, tearing along!
Thunderbolt engine, swift and strong,
Fifty tons she was, whole and sole!

I had been promoted to the express:
 I warrant you I was proud and gay,
It was the evening that ended May,
And the sky was a glory of tenderness.
We were thundering down to a midland town;
It makes no matter about the name—
For we never stopped there, or anywhere
For a dozen of miles on either side:
So it's all the same—

     Just there you slide,
With your steam shut off, and your brakes in hand
Down the steepest and longest grade in the land
At a pace that I promise you is grand.
We were just there with the express,
When I caught sight of a muslin dress
On the bank ahead; and as we passed—
You have no notion of how fast—
A girl shrank back from our baleful blast.

We were going a mile and a quarter a minute
With vans and carriages down the incline,
 But I saw her face, and the sunshine in it,
I looked in her eyes, and she looked in mine
 As the train went by, like a shot from a mortar,
A roaring hell-breath of dust and smoke;
And I mused for a moment, and then awoke,
 And she was behind us—a mile and a quarter.

And the years went on, and the express
 Leaped on in her black resistlessness,
 Evening by evening, England through.
Will—God rest rest him!—was found, a mash
Of bleeding rags, in a fearful smash
 He made with a Christmas train at Crewe.
It chanced I was ill the night of the mess,
 Or I shouldn't now be here alive;
But thereafter the five-o'clock out express
 Evening by evening I used to drive.

And I often saw her,—that lady I mean,
That I spoke of before. She often stood
A-top o' the bank: it was pretty high—
Say twenty feet, and backed by a wood.
 She would pick the daisies out of the green
To fling down at us as we went by.
We had got to be friends, that girl and I,
Though I was a rugged, stalwart chap,
And she a lady! I'd lift my cap,
Evening by evening, when I'd spy
That she was there, in the summer air,
Watching the sun sink out of the sky.

Oh, I didn't see her every night!
Bless you! no; just now and then,
  And not at all for a twelvemonth quite.
Then, one evening, I saw her again,
Alone, as ever, but deadly pale,
And down on the line, on the very rail,
  While a light, as of hell, from our wild wheels
    Tearing down the slope with their devilish clam-
                                    ors
And deafening din, as of giant's hammers
  That smote in a whirlwind of dust and smoke
All the instant or so that we sped to meet her.
Never, oh never, had she seemed sweeter!
I let yell the whistle, reversing the stroke
Down that awful incline, and signaled the guard
To put on their brakes, at once and hard—
Though we couldn't have stopped. We tattered
                                    the rail
Into splinters and sparks, but without avail.

We *couldn't* stop; and she wouldn't stir,
Saving to turn us her eyes, and stretch
Her arms to us;—and the desperate wretch
  I pitied, comprehending her.
So the brakes let off, and the steam full again,
Sprang down on the lady the terrible train—
She never flinched. We beat her down,
And ran on through the lighted length of the
                                    town
Before we could stop to see what was done.

Oh, I've run over more than one!
Dozens of 'em, to be sure, but none
That I pitied as I pitied her—
If I could have stopped, with all the spur
Of the train's weight on, and calmly—
But it wouldn't do with a lad like me
And she a lady—or had been—sir ?
Who was she? Best say no more of her!
The world is hard; but I'm her friend.
Stanch, sir,—down to the world's end.
It is a curl of her sunny hair
Set in this locket that I wear.
I picked it off the big wheel there.
Time's up, Jack. Stand clear, sir, Yes;
We're going out with the express.
                          —*W. Wilkins.*

LADY YEARDLEY'S GUEST.*

'Twas a Saturday night, mid-winter,
  And the snow with its sheeted pall
    Had covered the stubbled clearings
      That girdled the rude-built "Hall."
But high in the deep-mouthed chimney,
  'Mid laughter and shout and din,
    The children were piling yule-logs
      To welcome the Christmas in.

"Ah, so! We'll be glad to-morrow,"
  The mother, half musing, said,
As she looked at the eager workers,
  And laid on sunny head
A touch as of benediction—
  "For Heaven is just as near
The father at far Patuxent,
  As if he were with us here.

"So choose ye the pine and holly,
  And shake from the boughs the snow;
We'll garland the rough-hewn rafters
  As they garlanded long ago—

* (1654.)

Or ever Sir George went sailing†
  Away o'er the wild sea-foam—
In my beautiful English Sussex,
  The happy old walls at home."

She sighed: As she paused, a whisper
  Set quickly all eyes a-strain:
" *See! See!* "—and the boy's hand pointed—
  " *There's a face at the window-pane!* "
One instant a ghastly terror
  Shot sudden her features o'er;
The next, and she rose unblenching,
  And opened the fast-barred door.

" Who be ye that seek admission ?
  Who cometh for food and rest ?
This night is a night above others
  To shelter a straying guest."
Deep out of the snowy silence
  A guttural answer broke:
"I come from the great Three Rivers
  I am Chief of the Roan-oke."

Straight in through the frightened children,
  Unshrinking, the red man strode,
And loosed on the blazing hearthstone,
  From his shoulder, a light-borne load;
And out from the pile of deerskins,
  With look as serene and mild
As if it had been his cradle,
  Stepped softly a little child.

As he chafed at the fire his fingers,
  Close pressed to the brawny knee,
The gaze that the silent savage
  Bent on him was strange to see.
And then, with a voice whose yearning
  The father could scarcely stem,
He said—to the children pointing—
  " I want him to be like *them!*

"They weep for the boy in the wigwam
  I bring him, a moon of days,
To learn of the speaking paper,
  To hear of the wiser ways
Of the people beyond the water—
  To break with the plow the sod—
To be kind to papoose and woman—
  To pray to the white man's God."

" I give thee my hand!" And the Lady
  Pressed forward with sudden cheer;
" Thou shalt eat of my English pudding,
  And drink of my Christmas beer.
My sweethearts this night, remember,
  All strangers are kith and kin.
This night, when the dear Lord's Mother
  Could find no room at the inn! "

Next morn from the colony belfry
  Pealed gayly the Sunday chime,
And merrily forth the people
  Flocked, keeping the Christmas time.
And the Lady, with bright-eyed children
  Behind her, their limbs a-smile,
And the Chief in his skins and wampum,
  Came walking the narrow aisle.

Forthwith from the congregation
  Broke fiercely a sullen cry:
"Out! Out! *with the crafty red-skin!*
  Have at him! A spy! A spy! "
And quickly from belts leaped daggers,
  And swords from their sheaths flashed bare,
And men from their seats defiant
  Sprang, ready to slay him there.

†Sir George Yeardley, Governor of the Colony of
Virginia in 1626.

But facing the crowd with courage,
  As calm as a knight of yore,
Stepped bravely the fair-browed woman,
  The thrust of the steel before ;
And spake with a queenly gesture,
  Her hand on the Chief's brown breast,
  " *Ye dare not impeach my honor!*
  " *Ye dare not insult my guest!* "

They dropped at her words their weapons,
  Half shamed as the Lady smiled,
And told them the red man's story,
  And showed them the red man's child
And pledged them her broad plantations,
  That never would such betray
The trust that a Christian woman,
  Had shown on a Christmas day.
         —*Margaret J. Preston.*

"WHEN THE COWS COME HOME."

WITH klingle, klangle, klingle,
  Way down the dusty dingle,
  The cows are coming home ;
Now sweet and clear, and faint and low,
The airy twinklings come and go,
Like chimings from some far-off tower,
Or pattering of an April shower
    That makes the daisies grow ;
    Ko-ling, ko-ling, kolinglelingle,
    Way down the darkening dingle,
    The cows come slowly home ;
(And old-time friends, and twilight plays,
And starry nights and sunny days,
Come trooping up the misty ways,
    When the cows come home.)

With jingle, jangle, jingle,
  Soft tones that sweetly mingle,
  The cows are coming home ;
Malvine and Pearl and Florimel,
De Kamp, Redrose, and Gretchen Schell,
Queen Bess and Sylph, and Spangled Sue,
Across the fields I hear her ' 'loo-oo,''
    And clang her silver bell ;
    Go-ling, go-lang, golinglelingle,
    With faint, far sounds that mingle,
    The cows come slowly home ;
(And mother songs of long-gone years,
And baby-joys and childish tears,
And youthful hopes and youthful tears,
    When the cows come home.)

With ringle, rangle, ringle,
  By twos and threes and single.
  The cows are coming home ;
Through violet air we see the town,
And the summer sun aslipping down,
And the maple in the hazel glade
Throws down the path a longer shade,
    And the hills are growing brown.
    To-ring, to-rang, taringleringle,
    By threes, and fours and single.
    The cows come slowly home ;
(The same sweet sound of worldless psalm,
The same sweet June-day rest and calm,
The same sweet scent of bud and balm,
    When the cows come home.)

With tinkle, tankle, tinkle,
  Through fern and peri-winkle,
  The cows are coming home ;
A loitering in the checkered stream
Where the sun-rays glance and gleam,
Clarine, Peachbloom, and Phebe Phillis,
Stand knee-deep in the creamy lilies ;

In a drowsy dream,
To-link, to-lank, tolinklelinkle,
O'er banks with butter-cups atwinkle,
  The cows come slowly home ;
(And up through memory's dim ravine
Come the brook's old song and its old-time sheen,
And the cresent of the silver Queen,
  When the cows come home.)

With kingle, klangle, klingle,
  With loo-oo, and moo-oo and jingle,
  The cows are coming home ;
And over there on Merlin Hill
Hear the plaintive cry of the whip-poor-will,
And the dew-drops lie on the tangled vines,
And over the poplars Venus shines,
    And over the silent mill ;
    Ko-ling, ko-lang kolinglelingle,
    With a ting-a-ling and jingle,
    The cows come slowly home ;
(Let down the bars ; let in the train
Of long-gone songs, and flowers, and rain,
For dear old times come back again,
    When the cows come home.)
         —*Mrs. Agnes E. Mitchell.*

KARL, THE MARTYR.

IT was the closing of a summer's day
And trellis'd branches from encircling trees
Threw silver shadows o'er the golden space
Where groups of merry-hearted sons of toil
Were met to celebrate a village feast—
Casting away, in frolic sport, the cares
That ever press and crowd and leave their mark
Upon the brows of all whose bread is earned
By daily labor. 'Twas, perchance, the feast
Of fav'rite saint, or anniversary
Of one of bounteous Nature's season gifts
To grateful husbandry. Joy beamed forth
On ev'ry face, and the sweet echoes rang
With sounds of honest mirth, too rarely heard.

Somewhat apart from the assembled throng
There sat a swarthy giant, with a face
So nobly grand, that though (unlike the rest)
He joined not in their sports, but rather seemed
To please his eye with sight of others' joy.
There was a cast of sorrow on his brow,
As though it had been ever there. He sat
In listless attitude, yet not devoid
Of gentlest grace, as down his stalwart form
He bent, to catch the playful whisperings
And note the movements of a bright haired child
Who danced before him in the evening sun,
Holding a tiny brother by the hand.
He was the village smith (the rolled-up sleeves
And the well-charred leathern apron showed his
    craft),
Karl was his name, a man beloved by all.

He was not of the district. He had come
Among them ere his forehead bore one trace
Of age or suffering. A wife and child
He had brought with him ; but the wife was dead.
Not so children two who danced before him now,
So Karl was happy still that these two lived,
And laughed and danced before him in the sun.

The frolics pause : now Casper's laughing head
Rests wearily against his father's knee
In trusting lovingness, while Trudchen runs
To snatch a hasty kiss (the little man,
It may be, wonders if the tiny hand
With which he strives to reach his father's neck
Will ever grow so big and brown as that
He sees imbedded in his sister's curls) ;

When quick as lightning's flash up starts the
   smith,
Huddles the frightened children in his arms,
Thrusts them far back, extends his giant frame,
And covers them as with Goliath's shield.

Now hark! a rushing, yelping, panting sound,
So terrible that all stood chilled with fear;
And in the midst of that late joyous throng
Leapt an infurite hound, with flaming eyes,
Half-open mouth, and fiercely bristling hair,
Proving that madness drove the brute to death.
One spring from Karl, and the wild thing was
   seized,
Fast-prison'd in the stalwart Vulcan's grip.
A sharp, shrill cry of agony from Karl
Was mingled with the hound's low fevered growl,
And all, with horror, saw the creature's teeth
Fixed in the blacksmith's shoulder. None had
   power
To rescue him; for scarcely could you count
A moment's space ere both had disappeared—
The man and dog. The smith had leapt a fence,
And gained the forest with a frantic rush,
Bearing the hideous mischief in his arms.

A long receding cry came on the ear,
Showing how swift their flight, and fainter grew
The sound. Ere well a man had time to think
What might be done for help the sound was
   hushed—
Lost in the very distance; women crouched
And huddled up their children in their arms,
Men flew to seek their weapons—'twas a change
So swift and fearful none could realize
Its actual horrors for a time; but now,
The panic past, to rescue and pursuit.
Crash through the brake into the forest track;
But pitchy darkness, caused by closing night
And foliage dense, impedes the avengers' way,
When as they trip o'er something in their path—
It was the bleeding body of Karl
Warm, but quite dead. No other trace of Karl
Was near at hand; they called his name in vain,
They sought him in the forest all night through—
Living or dead he was not to be found.

At break of day they left the fruitless search.
Next morning, as an anxious village group
Stood meditating plans what best to do,
Came little Trudchen, who, in simple tones,
Said, "Father's at the forge, I heard him there
Working long hours ago, but he is angry;
I raised the latch; he bade me begone.
What have I done to make him chide me so?"
And then her bright blue eyes ran o'er with tears.
"The child's been dreaming through this troubled
   night,"
Said a kind dame, and drew the child toward her;
But the sad answers of the girl were such
As led them all to seek her father's forge.
It lay beyond the village some short span;
They forced the door, and there beheld the smith.
His sinewy frame was drawn to its full height,
And round his loins a double chain of iron,
Wrought with true workman skill, was riveted
Fast to an anvil of enormous weight.
He stood as pale and statue-like as death.
Now let his own words close the hapless tale.

"I killed the hound, you know, but not until
His maddening venom through my veins had
   passed;
I know full well the death in store for me,
And would not answer when you called my name,
But crouched among the brushwood while I
   thought
Over some plan. I know my giant strength,
And dare not trust it after reason's loss;
Why, I might turn and rend whom I most love.
I've made all fast now. 'Tis a hideous death.

I thought to plunge me in the deep, still pool
That skirts the forest, to avoid it; but
I thought that for the suicide's poor shift
I would not throw away my chance of heaven,
And meeting one who made earth heaven to me.
So I came home and forged these chains about
   me—
Full well I know no human hand can rend them—
And now am safe from harming those I love.
Keep off, good friends! Should God prolong my
   life,
Throw me such food as nature may require;
Look to my babies: *this* you are bound to do;
For by my deadly grasp that poor hound
How many of you have I saved from death
Such as *I* now await? But hence, away!
The poison works! These chains must try their
   strength;
My brain's on fire! With me 'twill soon be night.'

Too true his words: the brave, great-hearted
   Karl—
A raving maniac—battled with his chains
For three fierce days. The fourth day saw him
   free—
For Death's strong hand then loosed the martyr's
   bonds.

THE CRAZY KATE.

Go for a sail this mornin'? This way, yer honor,
   please.
Weather about? Lor' bless you, only a pleasant
   breeze;
My boat's out there in the harbor, and the man
   aboard's my mate;
Jump in, and I'll row you out, sir; that's her, the
   Crazy Kate.

Queer name for a boat, you fancy; well, so it is,
   maybe,
But Crazy Kate and her story's the talk o' the
   place, you see;
And me and my pardner knowed her—knowed
   her all her life—
We was both on us asked to the weddin' when she
   was made a wife.

Her as our boat's named arter was famous far and
   wide;
For years in all winds and weathers she haunted
   the harbor side.
With her great wild eyes a-starin' and a-strainin'
   across the waves,
Waitin' for what can't happen till the dead come
   out o' their graves.

She was married to young Ned Garling, a big
   brown fisher lad;
One week a bride, and the next one a sailor's
   widow—and mad.
It was one Christmas morning he made the lass
   his wife,
He'd a smile for all the lasses, but she loved him
   all her life.

A rollickin', gay young fellow, we thought her too
   good for him,
He'd been a bit wild and careless—but married
   all taut and trim.
We thought as he'd mend his manners when he
   won the village prize,
And carried her off in triumph before many a
   rival's eyes.

But one week wed and they parted—he went with
   the fisher fleet—
With the men who must brave the tempest that
   the women and bairns may eat.
It's a rough long life o' partin's is the life o' the
   fisher folk,
And there's never a winter passes but some good
   wife's heart is broke.

We've a sayin' among us sea folk as few on us dies
   in bed—
Walk through our little churchyard and read the
   tale of our dead—
It's mostly the bairns and the women as is restin'
   under the turf,
For half o' the men sleep yonder under the rollin'
   surf.

The night Kate lost her husband was the night o'
   the fearful gale—
She stood on the shore that mornin' and had
   watched the tiny sail
As it faded away in the distance—bound for the
   coast of France,
And the fierce wind bore it swiftly away from her
   anxious glance.

The boats that had sailed that mornin' with the
   fleet were half a score,
And never a soul among 'em came back to the
   English shore.
That New Year's Night was a sad one—the eyes of
   the women red
With weeping for brothers and husbands or
   fathers among the dead.

Kate heard it soon as any—the fate of her fisher
   lad—
But her eyes were wild and tearless; she went
   slowly and surely mad.
"He isn't drowned," she would murmur; "he
   will come again some day"—
And her lips shaped the self-same story as the
   long years crept away.

Spring and Summer and Autumn—in the fiercest
   Winter gale,
Would Crazy Kate stand watchin' for the glint of
   a far-off sail;
Stand by the hour together and murmur her hus-
   band's name—
For twenty years she watched there for the boat
   that never came.

She counted the years as nothin'—the shock that
   had sent her mad
Had left her love forever a brave, young, handsome lad;
She thought one day she should see him, just as
   he said good-bye,
When he leapt in his boat and vanished where
   the waters touched the sky.

She was but a lass when it happened—the last
   time I saw her there
The first faint streaks o' silver had come in her
   jet-black hair;
And then a miracle happened—her mad, weird
   words came right,
For the fisher lad came ashore, sir, one stormy
   New Year's Night.

We were all of us watchin', waitin', for at dusk
   we'd heard a cry,
A far-off cry, round the headland, and strained
   was every eye—
Strained through the deep'nin' darkness, and a
   boat was ready to man—
When, all of a sudden, a woman down to the surf-
   line ran.

'Twas Crazy Kate. In a moment, before what
   she meant was known,
The boat was out in the tempest—and she was in
   it alone.
She was out of sight in a second—but over the sea
   came a sound,
The voice of a woman cryin' that her long-lost
   love was found.

A miracle, sir, for the woman came back through
   the ragin' storm,
And there in the boat beside her was lyin' a lifeless form.
She leapt to the beach and staggered, cryin',
As the light of our lifted lanterns flashed on the
   face o' the dead.

It was him as had sailed away, sir—a miracle sure
   it seemed.
We looked at the lad and knowed him, and fan-
   cied we must ha' dreamed—
It was twenty years since we'd seen him—since
   Kate, poor soul, went mad,
But there in the boat that New Year's lay the
   same brown handsome lad.

Gently we took her from him—for she moaned
   that he was dead—
We carried him to a cottage and we laid him on a
   bed;
But Kate came pushin' her way through and she
   clasped the lifeless clay,
And we hadn't the heart to hurt her, so we
   couldn't tear her away.

The news of the miracle traveled, and folks came
   far and near,
And the woman talked of spectres—it had given
   'em quite a skeer;
And the parson he came with the doctor down to
   the cottage quick—
They thought as us sea-folks' fancy had played
   our eyes a trick.

But the parson, who'd known Kate's husband, as
   had married 'em in a church,
When he seed the dead lad's features he gave
   quite a sudden lurch,
And his face was as white as linen—for a moment
   it struck him dumb—
I half expected he'd tell us as the Judgment Day
   was come.

The Judgment Day, when the ocean, they say, 'll
   give up its dead;
What else meant those unchanged features,
   though twenty years had sped?

That night, with her arms around him, the poor
   mad woman died.
And here in our village churchyard we buried
   'em side by side.

'Twas the shock, they said, as killed her—the
   shock o' seein' him dead.
The story got in the papers, and far and near it
   spread;
And some only half believed it—I know what
   you'd say, sir; wait—
Wait till you hear the finish o' this story o' Crazy
   Kate.

It was all explained one mornin' as clear as the
   light o' day,
And when we knowed we were happy to think as
   she'd passed away,
As she died with her arms around him, her lips on
   the lips o' the dead—
Believin' the face she looked on was the face o'
   the man she'd wed.

But the man she'd wed was a villain, and that she
　never knew—
He hadn't been drowned in the tempest; he only
　of all the crew
Was saved by a French ship cruising and carried
　ashore, and there
Was nursed to life by a woman—a French girl,
　young and fair.

He fell in love with the woman—this dare-devil
　heartless Ned,
And married her, thinkin' the other had given
　him up for dead,
He was never the man—and we'd said so—for a
　lovin' lass like Kate;
But he mightn't ha' done what he did, sir, if he'd
　known of her cruel fate.

'Twas his son by the foreign woman, his image in
　build and face,
Whose lugger the storm had driven to his father's
　native place—
'Twas his son who had come like a phantom out
　of the long ago.
On the spot where Kate had suffered God's hand
　struck Ned the blow.

We learnt it all from the parson when Ned came
　over the waves
In search o' the son he worshiped—and he found
　two fresh-made graves.
Dang!—what was that? Sit steady? Rowed right
　into you, mate!
I forgot where I was for a moment—I was tellin'
　the gent about Kate.

　　　　　　　　　　—*George R. Sims.*

THE POLISH BOY.

WHENCE come those shrieks so wild and shrill,
　That cut, like blades of steel, the air,
Causing the creeping blood to chill
　With the sharp cadence of despair?

Again they come, as if a heart
　Were cleft in twain by one quick blow,
And every string had voice apart
　To utter its peculiar woe.

Whence came they? from yon temple, where
An altar, raised for private prayer,
Now forms the warrior's marble bed
Who Warsaw's gallant armies led.

The dim funereal tapers throw
A holy luster o'er his brow,
And burnish with their rays of light
The mass of curls that gather bright,
Above the haughty brow and eye
Of a young boy that's kneeling by.

What hand is that, whose icy press
　Clings to the dead with Death's own grasp,
But meets no answering caress?
　No thrilling fingers seek its clasp.
It is the hand of her whose cry
　Rang wildly, late, upon the air,
When the dead warrior met her eye
　Outstretched upon the altar there.

With pallid lip and stony brow
She murmurs forth her anguish now.
But hark! the tramp of heavy feet
Is heard along the bloody street;
Nearer and nearer yet they come,
With clanking eyes and noiseless drum.
Now whispered curses, low and deep
Around the holy temple creep;

The gate is burst, a ruffian band
Rush in and savagely demand,
With brutal voice and oath profane,
The startled boy for exile's chain.
The mother sprang with gesture wild,
And to her bosom clasped her child;
Then, with pale cheek and flashing eye,
Shouted with fearful energy,
"Back, ruffians, back! nor dare to tread
Too near the body of my dead;
Nor touch the living boy; I stand
Between him and your lawless band.
Take *me*, and bind these arms, these hands,
With Russia's heaviest iron bands,
And drag me to Siberia's wild
To perish, if 'twill save my child!"
"Peace, woman, peace!" the leader cried,
Tearing the pale boy from her side,
And in his ruffian grasp he bore
His victim at the temple door.
"One moment!" shrieked the mother: "one!
Will land or gold redeem my son?
Take heritage, take name, take all,
But leave him free from Russian thrall!
Take these!" and her white arms and hands
She stripped of rings and diamond bands,
And tore from braids of long black hair
The gems that gleamed like starlight there;
Her cross of blazing rubies last,
Down at the Russian's feet she cast.
He stooped to seize the glittering store;
Up springing from the marble floor,
The mother, with a cry of joy,
Snatched to her leaping heart the boy.
But no! the Russian's iron grasp
Again undid the mother's clasp.
Forward she fell, with one long cry
Of more than mortal agony.

But the brave child is roused at length,
　And breaking from the Russian's hold,
He stands, a giant in the strength
　Of his young spirit, fierce and bold.
Proudly he towers; his flashing eye,
　So blue and yet so bright,
Seems kindled from the eternal sky,
　So brilliant is its light.
His curling locks and crimson cheeks
Foretell the thought before he speaks;
With a voice full of proud command
He turned upon the wondering band;
"Ye told me not! no! no, nor can;
This hour has made the boy a man.
I knelt before my slaughtered sire,
Nor felt one throb of vengeful ire;
I wept upon his marble brow,
Yes, wept! I was a child; but now
My noble mother, on her knee,
Hath done the work of years for me!"
He drew aside his broidered vest,
And there, like slumbering serpent's crest,
The jeweled haft of poniard bright
Glittered a moment on the sight.
"Ha! start ye back? Fool! coward! knave!
Think ye my noble father's glaive
Would drink the life-blood of a slave?
The pearls that on the handle flame
Would blush to rubies in their shame;
The blade would quiver in thy breast
Ashamed of such ignoble rest.
No! thus I rend the tyrant's chain,
And fling him back a boy's disdain!"

A moment; and the funeral light
Flashed on the jeweled weapon bright;
Another, and his young heart's blood
Leaped to the floor, a crimson flood,
Quick to his mother's side he sprang,
And on the air his clear voice rang,
"Up, mother, up! I'm free! I'm free!
The choice was death or slavery.

Up, mother, up? Look on thy son!
It is freedom is forever won;
And now he waits one holy kiss
To bear his father home in bliss,
One last embrace, one blessing—one!
To prove thou knowest, approvest thy son,
What! silent yet? Canst thou not feel
My warm blood o'er my heart congeal?
Speak, mother, speak! lift up thy head!
What! silent still? Then art thou dead!
——Great God, I thank thee! Mother, I
Rejoice with thee—and thus—to die."
One long, deep breath, and his pale head
Lay on his mother's bosom—dead.
—*Ann S. Stephen.*

CURFEW MUST NOT RING TO-NIGHT.

England's sun was slowly setting
  O'er the hills so far away,
Filling all the land with beauty,
  At the close of one sad day;
And the last rays kiss'd the forehead
  Of a man and maiden fair,
He with step so slow and weakened,
  She with sunny, floating hair;
He with sad, bowed head, and thoughtful,
  She with lips so cold and white,
Struggling to keep back the murmur,
  "Curfew must not ring to-night."
"Sexton," Bessie's white lips faltered,
  Pointing to the prison old,
With its walls so dark and gloomy—
  Walls so dark, and damp, and cold—
"I've a lover in that prison,
  Doomed this very night to die
At the ringing of the Curfew,
  And no earthly help is nigh.
Cromwell will not come till sunset,"
  And her face grew strangely white,
As she spoke in husky whispers,
  "Curfew must not ring to-night."
"Bessie," calmly spoke the sexton—
  Every word pierced her young heart
Like a thousand gleaming arrows,
  Like a deadly poisoned dart—
"Long, long years I've rung the Curfew
  From that gloomy shadowed tower;
Every evening, just at sunset,
  It has told the twilight hour;
I have done my duty ever,
  Tried to do it just and right.
Now I'm old I will not miss it;
  Girl, the Curfew rings to-night!"
Wild her eyes and pale her features,
  Stern and white her thoughtful brow,
And within her heart's deep center
  Bessie made a solemn vow;
She had listened while the judges
  Read, without a tear or sigh,
"At the ringing of the Curfew—
  Basil Underwood *must die !*"
And her breath came fast and faster,
  And her eyes grew large and bright—
One low murmur scarcely spoken—
  "Curfew *must not* ring to-night!"
She with light step bounded forward,
  Sprang within the old church door,
Left the old man threading slowly
  Paths he'd trod so oft before,
Not one moment paused the maiden,
  But with cheek and brow aglow
Staggered up the gloomy tower,
  Where the bell swung to and fro;
Then she climbed the slimy ladder
  Dark, without one ray of light,
Upward still, her pale lips saying,
  "Curfew shall not ring to-night.
She has reached the topmost ladde.

O'er her hangs the great dark bell,
  And the awful gloom beneath her,
  Like the pathway down to hell;
See, the ponderous tongue is swinging,
  'Tis the hour of Curfew now,
And the sight has chilled her bosom,
  Stopped her breath and paled her brow
Shall she let it ring? No, never!
  Her eyes flash with sudden light,
As she springs and grasps it firmly—
  "Curfew shall not ring to-night!"
Out she swung, far out, the city
  Seemed a tiny speck below;
There, 'twixt heaven and earth suspended,
  As the bell swung to and fro,
And the half deaf sexton ringing
  (Years he had not heard the bell),
And he thought the twilight Curfew
  Rang young Basil's funeral knell;
Still the maiden clinging firmly,
  Cheek and brow so pale and white,
Stilled her frightened heart's wild beating—
  "Curfew shall not ring to-night."
It was o'er—the bell ceased swaying,
  And the maiden stepped once more
Firmly on the damp old ladder
  Where for hundred years before
Human foot had not been planted;
  And what she this night had done
Should be told in long years after—
  And the rays of setting sun
Light the sky with mellow beauty,
  Aged sires with heads of white
Tell their children why the Curfew
  Did not ring that one sad night.
O'er the distant hills came Cromwell;
  Bessie saw him, and her brow
Lately white with sickening terror,
  Glows with sudden beauty now;
At his feet she told her story,
  Showed her hands all bruised and torn;
And her sweet young face so haggard,
  With a look so sad and worn,
Touched his heart with sudden pity
  Lit his eyes with misty light;
"Go! your lover lives," cried Cromwell,
  "Curfew shall not ring to-night!"
       —*Rose Hartwick Thorpe.*

THE BURNING PRAIRIE.

The prairie stretched as smooth as a floor,
  As far as the eye could see,
And the settler sat at his cabin door,
  With his little girl on his knee;
Striving her letters to repeat,
And pulling her apron over her feet.

His face was wrinkled but not old,
  For he bore an upright form,
And his shirt sleeves back to the elbow rolled,
  They showed a brawny arm,
And near in the grass with toes upturned,
Was a pair of old shoes, cracked and burned.

A dog with his head betwixt his paws,
  Lay lazily dozing near,
Now and then snapping his tar black jaws
  At the fly that buzzed in his ear;
And near was the cow-pen, made of rails,
And a bench that held two milk pails.

In the open door an ox-yoke lay,
  The mother's old redoubt,
To keep the little one, at her play
  On the floor, from falling out;
While she swept the hearth with a turkey wing,
And filled her tea-kettle at the spring.

The little girl on her father's knee.
With eyes so bright and blue,
From A, B, C, to X, Y, Z,
Had said her lesson through;
When a wind came over the prairie land,
And caught the primer out of her hand.

The watch-dog whined, the cattle lowed
And tossed their horns about,
The air grew gray as if it snowed,
"There will be a storm, no doubt,"
So to himself the settler said:
"But, father, why is the sky so red?"

The little girl slid off his knee,
And all of a tremble stood;
"Good wife," he cried, "come out and see,
The skies are as red as blood."
"God save us!" cried the settler's wife,
"The prairie's a-fire, we must run for life!"

She caught the baby up, "Come, come,
Are ye mad? to your heels, my man;"
He followed, terror-stricken, dumb,
And so they ran and ran.
Close upon them was the snort and swing
Of buffaloes madly galloping.

The wild wind, like a sower sows
The ground with sparkles red;
And the flapping wings of the bats and crows,
And the ashes overhead,
And the bellowing deer, and the hissing snake
What a swirl of terrible sounds they make!

No gleam of the river water yet,
And the flames leap on and on
A crash and a fiercer whirl and jet,
And the settler's house is gone.
The air grows hot; "This fluttering curl
Would burn like flax," said the little girl.

And as the smoke against her drifts,
And the lizard slips close by her,
She tells how the little cow uplifts
Her speckled face from the fire;
For she cannot be hindered from looking back
At the fiery dragon on their track.

They hear the crackling grass and sedge,
The flames as they whir and rave,
On, on! they are close to the water's edge,—
They are breast deep in the wave;
And lifting their little one high o'er the tide,
"We are saved, thank God, we are saved!" they
cried.   —*Alice Carey.*

THE LIFEBOAT.

BEEN out in the lifeboat often? Ay, ay, sir, oft
enough
When it's rougher than this? Lor' bless you! this
ain't what *we* calls rough!
It's when there's a gale a-blowin', and the waves
run in and break
On shore with a roar like thunder and the white
cliffs seem to shake;
When the sea is a hell of waters, and the bravest
holds his breath
As he hears the cry for the lifeboat—his summons,
maybe, to death—
That's when we call it rough, sir; but, if we can
get her afloat,
There's always enough brave fellows ready to
man the boat.

You've heard of the Royal Helen, the ship as was
wrecked last year?
Yon be the rock she struck on—the boat as went
out be here;
The night as she struck was reckoned the worst as
ever we had,
And this is a coast in winter where the weather be
awful bad.
The beach here was strewed with wreckage, and
to tell you the truth, sir, then
Was the only time as ever we'd a bother to get the
men.
The single chaps was willin', and six of 'em volun-
teered,
But most on us here is married, and the wives that
night was skeered.

Our women ain't chicken-hearted when it comes
to savin' lives,
But death that night looked certain—and our
wives be only wives;
Their lot ain't bright at the best, sir; but here,
when the man lies dead,
'Tain't only a husband missin', it's the children's
daily bread;
So our women began to whimper and beg o' the
chaps to stay—
I only heerd on it after, for that night I was kept
away.
I was up at my cottage, yonder, where the wife lay
nigh her end,
She'd been ailin' all the winter, and nothin' 'ud
make her mend.

The doctor had given her up, sir, and I knelt by
her side and prayed,
With my eyes as red as a babby's, that Death's
hand might yet be stayed.
I heerd the wild wind howlin', and I looked on the
wasted form,
And thought of the awful shipwreck as had come
in the ragin' storm;
The wreck of my little homestead—the wreck of
my dear old wife,
Who'd sailed with me forty years, sir, o'er the
troublous waves of life.
And I looked at the eyes so sunken, as had been
my harbor lights,
To tell of the sweet home haven in the wildest
darkest nights.

She knew she was sinkin' quickly—she knew as
her end was nigh,
But she never spoke o' the troubles as I knew on
her heart must lie,
For we'd had one great big sorrow with Jack, our
only son—
He'd got into trouble in London, as lots o' the lads
ha' done;
Then he'd bolted, his masters told us—he was
allus what folk call wild,
From the day as I told his mother, her dear face
never smiled.
We heerd no more about him, we never knew
where he went,
And his mother pined and sickened for the message he never sent.

I had my work to think of; but she had her grief
to nurse,
So it eat away at her heartstrings, and her health
grew worse and worse.
And the night as the Royal Helen went down on
yonder sands,
I sat and watched her dyin', holdin' her wasted
hands.
She moved in her doze a little, then her eyes were
opened wide,
And she seemed to be seekin' somethin', as she
looked from side to side;

Then half to herself she whispered. "Where's
   Jack, to say good-bye?
It's hard not to see my darlin', and ask him afore
   I die!"

I was stoopin' to kiss and soothe her, while the
   tears ran down my cheek,
And my lips were shaped to whisper the words I
   couldn't speak,
When the door of the room burst open, and my
   mates were there outside
With the news that the boat was launchin'.
   "You're wanted!" their leader cried.
"You've never refused to go, John; you'll put
   these cowards right.
There's a dozen of lives maybe, John, as lie in our
   hands to-night!"
'Twas old Ben Brown, the captain; he laughed at
   the women's doubt.
We'd always been first on the beach, sir, when the
   boat was goin' out.

I didn't move, but I pointed to the white face on
   the bed—
"I can't go, mate," I murmured; "in an hour she
   may be dead.
I cannot go and leave her to die in the night
   alone."
As I spoke Ben raised his lantern, and the light on
   my wife was thrown;
And I saw her eyes fixed strangely with a pleading look on me.
While a tremblin' finger pointed through the door
   to the ragin' sea.
Then she beckoned me near, and whispered, "Go,
   and God's will be done!
For every lad on that ship, John, is some poor
   mother's son."

Her head was full of the boy, sir—she was thinking, maybe, some day
For lack of a hand to help him his life might be
   cast away.
"Go, John, and the Lord watch o'er you! and spare
   me to see the light,
And bring you safe," she whispered, "out of the
   storm to-night."
Then I turned and kissed her softly, and tried to
   hide my tears.
And my mates outside, when they saw me, set up
   three hearty cheers;
But I rubbed my eyes wi' my knuckles, and turned
   to old Ben and said,
"I'll see her again maybe, lad, when the sea gives
   up its dead."

We launched the boat in the tempest, though death
   was the goal in view,
And never a one but doubted if the craft could
   live it through;
But our boat she stood it bravely, and, weary and
   wet and weak,
We drew in hail of the vessel we had dared so
   much to seek.
But just as we come upon her she gave a fearful
   roll,
And went down in the seethin' whirlpool with
   every livin' soul!
We rowed for the spot, and shouted, for all around
   was dark—
But only the wild wind answered the cries from
   our plungin' bark.

I was strainin' my eyes and watchin', when I
   thought I heard a cry,
And I saw past our bows a somethin' on the crest
   of a wave dashed by;
I stretched out my hand to seize it. I dragged it
   aboard and then
I stumbled, and struck my forrud, and fell like a
   log on Ben.

I remember a hum of voices, and then I knowed
   no more
Till I came to my senses here, sir—here, in my
   home ashore.
My forrud was tightly bandaged, and I lay on my
   little bed—
I'd slipped, so they told me arter, and a rulluck
   had struck my head.

Then my mates came in and whispered; they'd
   heard I was comin' round,
At first I could scarcely hear 'em, it seemed like a
   buzzin' sound;
But as soon as my head got clearer, and accustomed to hear 'em speak,
I knew as I'd lain like that, sir, for many a long,
   long week,
I guessed what the lads was hidin' for their poor
   old shipmate's sake.
I could see by their puzzled faces they'd got some
   news to break;
So I lifts my head from the pillow, and I says to
   old Ben, "Look here!
I'm able to bear it now, lad—tell me, and never
   fear."

Not one on 'em ever answered, but presently Ben
   goes out,
And the others slink away like, and I says, "What's
   this about?
Why can't they tell me plainly as the poor old
   wife is dead?"
Then I fell again on the pillows, and I hid my
   achin' head;
I lay like that for a minute, till I heard a voice cry
   "John!"
And I thought it must be a vision as my weak eyes
   gazed upon;
For there by the bedside, standin' up and well was
   my wife.
And who do ye think was with her? Why, Jack,
   as large as life.

It was him as I'd saved from drownin' the night
   as the lifeboat went
To the wreck of the Royal Helen; 'twas that as
   the vision meant.
They'd brought us ashore together, he'd knelt by
   his mother's bed,
And the sudden joy had raised her like a miracle
   from the dead;
And mother and son together had nursed me back
   to life,
And my old eyes woke from darkness to look on
   my son and wife.
Jack? He's our right hand now, sir; 'twas Providence pulled him through—
He's allus the first aboard her when the lifeboat
   wants a crew

               —*George R. Sims.*

ASLEEP AT THE SWITCH.

THE first thing that I remember was Carlo tugging
   away,
With the sleeve of my coat fast in his teeth, pulling as much as to say
"Come, master, awake, and tend to the switch,
   lives now depend upon you:
Think of the souls in the coming train and the
   graves your sending them to;
Think of the mother and babe at her breast, think
   of the father and son.
Think of the lover, and loved one, too, think of
   them doomed every one
To fall, as it were, by your very hand, into you
   fathomless ditch.
Murdered by one who should guard them from
   harm, who now lies asleep at the switch."

I sprang up amazed, scarce knew where I stood,
  sleep had o'er mastered me so;
I could hear the wind hollowly howling and the
  deep river dashing below,
I could hear the forest leaves rustling as the trees
  by the tempest were fanned;
But what was that noise at a distance? That I
  could not understand!
I heard it at first indistinctly, like the rolling of
  some muffled drum,
Then nearer and nearer it came to me, and made
  my very ears hum;
What is this light that surrounds me and seems to
  set fire to my brain?
What whistle's that yelling so shrilly! Oh, God! I
  know now—it's the train.

We often stand facing some danger, and seem to
  take root at the place;
So I stood with this demon before me, its heated
  breath scorching my face;
Its headlight made day of the darkness, and
  glared like the eye of some witch;
The train was almost upon me, before I remembered the switch.
I sprang to it, seizing it wildly, the train dashing
  fast down the track—
The switch resisted my efforts, some devil seemed
  holding it back;
On, on, came the fiery-eyed monster and shot by
  my face like a flash;
I swooned to the earth the next moment, and
  knew nothing after the crash.

How long I laid there unconscious 'twere impos-
  sible for me to tell.
My stupor was almost a heaven, my waking almost
  a hell—
For I then heard the piteous moaning and shriek-
  ing of husbands and wives,
And I thought of the day we all shrink from, when
  I must account for their lives;
Mothers rushed like maniacs, their eyes staring
  madly and wild;
Fathers, losing their courage, gave way to their
  grief like a child;
Children searching for parents, I noticed, as by
  me they sped,
And lips that could form naught but "Mamma,"
  were calling for one perhaps dead.

My mind was made up in a second, the river
  should hide me away;
When, under the still burning rafters, I suddenly
  noticed there lay
A little white hand, she who owned it was doubt-
  less an object of love
To one whom her loss would drive frantic, tho' she
  guarded him now from above;
I tenderly lifted the rafters and quietly laid them
  one side;
How little was the thought of her journey, when she
  left for this last fatal ride;
I lifted the log from off her, and while searching for some spark of life,
Turned her little face up in the starlight, and
  recognized—Maggie, my wife!

Oh, Lord! Thy scourge is a hard one, at a blow
  Thou has shattered my pride;
My life will be one endless night-time, with
  Maggie away from my side;
How often we've sat down and pictured the
  scenes in our long happy life;
How I'd strive through all my life-time to build
  up a home for my wife,
How people would envy us always in our cozy
  and neat litte nest;
When I would do all the labor, and Maggie should
  all the day rest;

How one of God's blessings might cheer us, when
  some day I p'r'aps should be rich.
But all of my dreams have been shattered while I
  lay there asleep at the switch.

I fancied I stood on my trial, the jury and judge I
  could see,
And every eye in the court room was steadfastly
  fixed upon me,
And fingers were pointed in scorn, till I felt my
  face blushing red;
And the next thing I heard were the words,
  "Hung by the neck until dead."
Then I felt myself pulled once again, and my
  hand caught tight hold of a dress,
And I heard, "What's the matter, dear Jim?
  You've had a bad nightmare I guess."
And there stood Maggie, my wife, with never a
  scar from the ditch.
I'd been taking a nap in my bed and had not been
  asleep at the switch.

THE GREAT TEMPTATION.

His love was mine no more, mother; I saw it in
  his eyes;
I did not heed his tender words, I knew that they
  were lies;
I could not be deceived, mother; my love had
  made me wise.

You wondered why my cheek was pale; I would
  not tell a lie;
And yet, how could I speak the truth which almost made me die?
So I lay on your heart and cried, mother, an ex-
  ceeding bitter cry.

A maiden's heart is lightly won—he won mine in
  a day;
How could I know he wanted it to break and cast
  away?
He had such a noble face, mother, and yet he
  could betray.

My world had never seemed so fair—he was the
  world to me;
I feared no future day, because my only future
  he;
I fled to him as to my rest, and loved him ut-
  terly.

There are who pray: "From sudden death de-
  liver us, good Lord."
I dare not pray that awful prayer, lest God should
  take me at my word,
And send me awful lingering, with pains of death
  deferred.

I saw the rosy dawn, mother, cloud over
  gradually;
I saw the shadows deepen, and the last sunbeam
  fly;
And then I said, "It is enough; would God that I
  could die!"

He came at last to blame himself for having long
  delayed;
I must not think he loved me less—"No, surely,
  no," he said;
He kissed me with a Judas kiss; I felt myself betrayed.

I would be strong. I would live on, and in the end
forget;
But sometimes in the night I woke and found my
pillow wet,
And knew that all my years to come would be a
long regret.

Soon tidings came that turned my love to gall and
wounded pride;
He who had knelt, and sworn to love me only,
none beside,
Had pledged his perjured word again, and won
another bride.

I hated him, I hated her; I hugged my misery;
I writhed against God, earth, and heaven; I
cursed my sunless sky.
"They shall not build their bliss," I cried, "upon
my agony!"

Then came a day, from weariness I slept till after
dawn,
And started at the clang of bells—it was the bridal
morn;
The whole world seemed to keep a feast, and I
was so forlorn.

I watched the clock, I told each beat, and as the
hours went by,
I knew I must have cherished hope for some hope
seemed to die;
They to be building up their bliss upon my
misery.

I would go gliding up the church, right to the
altar-stair,
And steal, a spectre, to the feast and break upon
the prayer,
And throw him back his ring, in sight of all the
people there.

Small pity had he had for me, that I should spare
his bride;
Nay, I would laugh to see the girl grow pallid at
his side.
No mercy had been shown to me, I would show
none, I cried.

Then quick as thought my cruel thought, I rush'd
into the street,
And pluck'd my shawl about my face, and never
turned to greet,
But passed like Vengeance, through the crowd,
with evil-winged feet.

The solemn, solemn church, it soothed and
healed me unaware;
The holy light came flooding in, like balm on my
despair;
How could I harbor evil thoughts when Jesus
Christ was there?

And then I heard the organ peal—no gorgeous
burst of sound,
But a low, pleading human voice, soul-thrilling,
passion-bound,
That seemed to say, "My child is dead; behold,
the lost is found!"

I looked upon her face, poor bride! so young, so
true, so fair,
And blushing, half with love and half to see the
people stare;
I sank my shafts, I hid my face, and clasped my
hands in prayer.

I heard their vows, I heard his voice, I heard the
priest who prayed.
I suffered still, but, Christ be praised! the thun-
der-storm was laid;
God had said, "Peace, be still," said lo! the stormy
heart obeyed.

Through tears I looked upon my love, in sadness,
not in hate;
It was not he that worked my woe—not he, but
only Fate;
Sorrowing, not sinful, bruised, not lost, I left the
church's gate.
—*Alice Horton.*

A SCAR ON THE FACE.

She was drunk—mad drunk—was Molly, the night
that I saw her first;
I'd seen some terrible cases, but her's was the
very worst.
This Refuge had just been started for the daugh-
ters of night and sin,
And I was the Matron here, sir, on the night that
they brought her in.

Her face was crushed and swollen, and a blow
had cut her eye,
And the blood that had oozed unnoticed on her
cheek was caked and dry.
She laughed with a hoarse, wild laughter, and
capered and kicked about,
And she swore and she cursed so foully, we
thought we must turn out.

She'd come for a spree, as often these poor lost
creatures come,
They hear of our "midnight meetings" away in
their filthy slum;
I've seen 'em jump on the platform and fling down
the chairs and shriek,
And join in a ribald chorus when the clergyman
tried to speak.

But Molly was worse than any—she staggered
across the place
And picked up a brass-bound hymn-book and
aimed at our chaplain's face;
It cut him across the cheek-bone, and he uttered
a cry of pain,
Then we rushed at Molly to seize her, but she
struggled with might and main.

She bit and she tore and she scratched us, and
kicked liked a beast at bay,
Then all of a sudden reeled forward and still as a
mouse she lay;
In the struggle her wound was injured, and the
blood flowed down apace,
And the same sort of mark, we noticed, was on
hers and the chaplain's face.

What a fist had done for Molly a hymn-book had
done for him;
He was only a young beginner, and he trembled
in every limb,
For the wound was deep and painful; but he
pushed his way through the crowd,
And cleared his voice with an effort, and spoke
these words aloud:

"Poor lass, may the Lord forgive her as I forgive
her, too!"
And silent, as if by magic, stood the whole of the
yelling crew;
While he, with his face all bleeding, did the words
of the Savior quote,
That the left cheek should be offered to one who
the right cheek smote.

He came where we held the wanton, and he
  moved his lips in prayer,
And smoothed from her bloody features the
  masses of tangled hair;
" Take her away," he whispered, " and see that
  her wound is drest ; "
Then he spake aloud the blessing, and then he
  dismissed the rest.

We kept the girl at the Refuge right from the
  hour she swooned
Till time and a kindly surgeon had thoroughly
  healed the wound ,
In a week it was closed completely, but leaving a
  mark to mar,
And the face of the poor lost creature and his had
  the self-same scar.

The day she was well she left us—left us with
  never a word ;
Went back to the awful outcasts with whom such
  women herd ;
And now and again we gathered news of the life
  she led ;
" In the hospital " once, they told us, and then
  that the girl was dead.

It was five years after that, sir; one night went
  our faithful priest
On a mission of love and mercy to an awful place
  down East—
To a den where the lowest women herd with the
  vilest thieves—
They're some of the very worst, sir, that our
  Refuge, here, receives.

He'd heard from a girl who came here tales of
  this devil's place,
And he made up his mind to storm it, armed with
  the Word of Grace.
His face was flushed and red as he told us, and
  spoke of the souls to win,
And the task that the Lord had sent him in that
  haven of shame and sin.

He laughed when we spoke of danger, and that
  night went forth alone—
But we had a strange misgiving which we hardly
  liked to own ;
He was back on the stroke of midnight—back
  from the jaws of hell,
But his face was pale and ghastly ; he'd a strange,
  wild tale to tell.

He had entered that fearful alley and spoken
  God's word aloud,
Till the people swarmed about him in a thick and
  threatening crowd ;
And they jeered and they spat and hooted, and
  the women were worst of all,
For they picked up filth to pelt him, and drove
  him against the wall.

Beaten and bruised and smothered, he then would
  have turned and fled,
When a well-aimed brickbat struck him full on
  his hatless head ;
Then he turned quite sick and giddy, and felt
  himself dragged along,
And a door was slammed in the faces of the
  threatening, murderous throng.

And beside him there stood a woman—he could
  hardly see her face,
For a foul and noisome darkness hung o'er the
  dreadful place.
" Hush for your life!" she whispered. " I've
  bolted and barred the door;
They'd 'ave your blood if I'd let 'em—hark how
  the tigers roar!

" They found out as you're the parson as 'tices
  the gals away ;
They say it's through you they peaches and goes
  on the ' Christian ' lay.
I dragged you in here and saved you, and sent out
  a gal for the ' cops ; '
Ha, they're a-comin', sir! Listen! the noise and
  the shoutin' stops."

The noise was changed in a moment to a hiss and
  a sullen groan ;
The woman crept close and listened, then open
  the door was thrown,
And there was a sergeant standing with six of his
  tallest men,
And our chaplain walked between them out of
  that awful den.

And just as they reached the entry, lo, a woman's
  piercing shriek
Told of the brutal vengeance the ruffians tried to
  wreak.
He guessed what it was, did the sergeant, and
  hurrying back they found
The woman who'd saved our chaplain all of a
  heap on the ground.

The crowd in their brutal fury had beaten the
  woman down.
They kicked at her prostrate body till the red
  blood stained her gown,
But nobody knew who'd done it—the cowards had
  slunk away ;
Her face was all white and ghastly in the light of
  the bull's-eye's ray.

'Twas the face of an old acquaintance our chaplain saw that night ;
By the scar on the cheek he knew her, in the
  lantern's quivering light—
'Twas Molly, the long lost Molly, the girl that we
  thought was dead—
She beckoned him down and whispered, and these
  were the words she said ;

" I know'd yer to-night by yer scar, the scar o'
  the cut I made ;
I heerd how yer treated me then, sir—how yer
  give me yer blessin' and prayed.
And I sez when I see yer in danger, 'Moll, you've
  got a debt to pay.'
So I dragged yer away in yonder, and I 'eld them
  curs at bay."

Died ? No, she didn't : we saved her—she's
  matron here under me ;
That's she—and ah, here comes the chaplain—now
  both the scars you can see.
And often we tell the story how the Lord in his
  tender grace
Saved a life and a soul together, all through a
  scar on the face.
                              —*George R. Sims.*

THE BLACKSMITH'S STORY

WELL, no ; my wife ain't dead, sir,
  But I've lost her all the same ;
She left me voluntarily,
  And neither was to blame.
It's rather a queer story,
  And I think you will agree,
When you hear the circumstances
  'Twas rather rough on me.

She was a soldier's widow.
  He was killed at Malvern Hill;
And when I married her she seemed
  To sorrow for him still;
But I brought her here to Kansas,
  And I never want to see
A better wife than Mary was
  For five bright years to me.

The change of scene brought cheerfulness,
  And soon a rosy glow
Of happiness warmed Mary's cheeks
  And melted all their snow.
I think she loved me some—I'm bound
  To think that of her, sir,
And as for me—I can't begin
  To tell how I loved her!

Three years ago the baby came
  Our humble home to bless,
And then I reckon I was nigh
  To perfect happiness;
'Twas hers—'twas mine; but no language
  Have I to explain to you
How that little girl's weak fingers
  Our hearts together drew.

Once we watched it through a fever,
  And with each gasping breath,
Dumb, with an awful wordless woe,
  We waited for its death;
And, though I'm not a pious man,
  Our souls together there,
For Heaven to spare our darling,
  Went up in voiceless prayer.

And when the doctor said 'twould live,
  Our joy what words could tell?
Clasped in each other's arms we stood,
  And our grateful tears fell.
Sometimes, you see, the shadow fell
  Across our little nest,
But it only made the sunshine seem
  A doubly welcome guest.

Work came to me a plenty,
  And I kept the anvil ringing—
Early and late you'd find me there,
  A-hammering and singing;
Love nerved my arm to labor,
  And moved my tongue to song,
And though my singing wasn't sweet,
  It was tremendous strong.

One day a one-armed stranger stopped
  To have me nail a shoe,
And while I was at work we passed
  A compliment or two;
I asked him how he lost his arm.
  He said 'twas shot away
At Malvern Hill. "At Malvern Hill!
  Did you know Robert May?"

"That's me," said he. "You, you!" I gasped,
  Choking with horrid doubt;
"If you're the man, just follow me;
  We'll try this mystery out!"
With dizzy steps I led him to
  My Mary. God! 'twas true!
Then the bitterest pangs of misery
  Unspeakable I knew.

Frozen with deadly horror,
  She stared with eyes of stone,
And from her quivering lips there broke
  One wild despairing moan.
'Twas he! the husband of her youth,
  Now risen from the dead.
But all too late—and with bitter cry,
  Reeling, her senses fled.

What could be done? He was believed
  As dead. On his return
He strove in vain some tidings
  Of his absent wife to learn.
'Twas well that he was innocent,
  Else I'd have killed him, too,
So dead he never would have riz
  Till Gabriel's trumpet blew!

It was agreed that Mary then
  Between us should decide,
And each by her decision
  Would sacredly abide.
No sinner at the judgment-seat,
  Waiting eternal doom,
Could suffer what I then did,
  Waiting sentence in that room.

Rigid and breathless there we stood,
  With nerves as tense as steel,
While Mary's eyes sought each white face
  In piteous appeal.
God! could not woman's duty
  Be less hardly reconciled
Between her lawful husband
  And the father of her child?

Ah! how my heart was chilled to ice,
  When she knelt down and said:
"Forgive me, John! 'Tis my husband
  Here—alive, not dead!"
I raised her tenderly, and tried
  To tell her she was right,
But somehow in my aching breast
  The prisoned words stuck tight.

"But, John, I can't leave baby!"
  "What! wife and child!" cried I.
"Must I yield all! Ah, cruel fate!
  Better that I should die.
Think of the long, sad, lonely hours
  Waiting in gloom for me—
No wife to cheer me with her love,
  No babe to climb my knee!

"And yet you are her mother,
  And the sacred mother love
Is still the purest, tenderest tie
  That Heaven ever wove.
Take her, but promise, Mary—
  For that will bring no shame—
My little girl bear and learn
  To lisp her father's name!"

It may be, in the life to come,
  I'll meet my child and wife;
But yonder, by my cottage gate,
  We parted for this life;
One long hand clasp from Mary,
  And my dream of love was done—
One long embrace from baby,
  And my happiness was gone!
              —Frank Olive.

A BUNCH OF PRIMROSES.

I am only a faded primrose, dying for want of air;
I and my drooping sisters lie in a garret bare.
We were plucked from the pleasant woodland
  only a week ago,
But our leaves have lost their beauty and our
  heads are bending low.

We grew in a yellow cluster under a shady tree,
In a spot where the winds came wooing straight
  from the Sussex sea;
And the brisk breeze kissed us boldly as we nod-
  ded to and fro
In the smiling April weather—only a week ago.

Only a week this morning! Ah me! but it seems
  a year
Since the only dew on our petals was a woman's
  briny tear;
Since the breeze and the merry sunshine were
  changed for this stifling gloom
And the soot of the smoky chimneys that robs us
  of our bloom.

We grew in a nook so quiet, behind a hedge so
  high;
We were hid from the peeping children,' who,
  laughing, passed us by;
But a primrose gatherer spied us—his cruel hand
  came down;
We were plucked in the early morning, and packed
  and sent to town.

We were tossed in a busy market from grimy
  hand to hand,
Till a great rough woman took us and hawked us
  through the Strand;
Clutched in her dirty fingers our tender stalks
  were tied,
And "A penny a bunch, who'll buy 'em—fine primroses!" she cried.

We lay on a woman's basket till a white-faced
  girl came past;
There was, O, such a world of yearning in the
  lingering look she cast—
Cast on the tumbled bunches—a look that seemed
  to say,
"O, if I only had you!"—but she sighed and she
  turned away.

She was only gone a moment, and then she was
  back again;
She'd the look on her pale, pinched features that
  told of the hunger pain;
She held in her hand the penny that ought to have
  bought her bread,
But she dropped it into the basket and took us
  home instead.

Home—how we seemed to wither, as the light of
  day grew dim,
And up to a London garret she bore us with
  weary limb!
But her clasp it was kind and gentle, and there
  shone a light in her eyes
That made us think for a moment we were under
  our native skies.

She stole in the room on tiptoe, and "Alice," she
  softly said,
"See what I've brought you, Alice!" Then a sick
  girl raised her head,
And a faint voice answered, "Darling, how kind
  of you to bring
The flowers I love so dearly—I've longed for them
  all this spring.

"I've thought of it so often, the green hills far
  away,
And the posies we used to gather—it seems but
  the other day;
Lay them beside my pillow, they'll last as long as
  I—
How quickly in cruel London the country blos-
  soms die!"

We pined in our gloomy prison, and we thought
  how sweet we were
Blooming among the hedgerows out in the balmy
  air,
Where we gladdened the eyes that saw us in all
  our yellow pride,
And we thought how our lives were wasted as we
  lay by a sick-bedside.

We thought how our lives were wasted until we
  grew to know
We were dear to the dying workgirl for the sake
  of the long ago;
That her anguish was half forgotten as she looked
  upon us and went
Back in her dreams to the woodland filled with
  the primrose scent.

We primroses are dying, and so is Alice, fast;
But her sister sits besides her, watching her to the
  last,
Working with swollen eyelids for the white slave's
  scanty wage,
And starving to save her darling and to still the
  fever's rage.

We stand on the little table beside the sick girl's
  bed,
And we know by the words she murmurs that she
  wanders in her head;
She stretches her hand to take us, and laughs like
  a child at play—
She thinks that she sees us growing on the old
  bank far away.

Forgotten the gloomy garret, the fierce and the
  fevered strife—
Forgotten the weary journey that is ending with
  her life;
The black, black night has vanished, and the
  weary workgirl hies
Back to her country childhood, plucking a primrose prize.

We have banished awhile her sorrow, we have
  brought back a sunny smile
That belongs to the children's faces in the days
  that are free from guile,
The Babylon roar comes floating up from the
  street below;
Yet she lists to the gentle plashing of a brook in
  its Spring-tide flow.

The gurgling brook in the meadow, with the
  primrose-laden brim—
How thick were the yellow clusters on the bank
  where she sat with him;
With him who had loved and lost her, who had
  trampled a blossom down,
Ah me! for the country blossoms brought to the
  cruel town!

Thank God for the good brave sister who found
  the lost one there;
Who toiled with her for the pittance that paid for
  that garret bare;
Who slaved when the wasted fingers grew all too
  weak to sew,
And hid all her troubles bravely that Alice might
  never know.

We have brought one country sunbeam to shine
  in that garret bare;
But to-morrow will see us lifeless—killed by the
  poisoned air.
Then the primrose dream will vanish, and Alice
  will ask in vain
For the poor little yellow posy that made her a
  child again.

  *   *   *   *   *   *

On to our faded petals there falls a scalding tear,
As we lie to-night on the bosom of her who held us
  dear;
We shall go to the grave together—for the workgirl lies at rest,
With a faded primrose posy clasped to her icy
  breast.

—George R. Sims.

THE RUINED MERCHANT.

A COTTAGE home and sloping lawn, and trellised
   vines and flowers,
And little feet to chase away the rosy-fingered
   hours;
A fair young face to part at eve the shadows in
   the door;—
I picture thus a home I knew in happy days of
   yore.

Says one, a cherub thing of three, with childish
   heart elate,
" Papa is *tomin'*, let me *do* to meet *'im* at te
   date ! "
Another takes the music up, and flings it on the
   air,
" Papa has come, but why so slow his footstep on
   the stair ? "

" O father! did you bring the books I've waited
   for so long,
The baby's rocking-horse and drum, and mother's
   ' Angel Song ?
And did you see "—but something holds the ques-
   tioning lips apart,
And something settles very still upon that joyous
   heart.

The quick-discerning wife bends down with her
   white hand to stay
The clouds from tangling with the curls that on
   his forehead lay,
To ask, in gentle tones, " Beloved, by what rude
   tempest tossed ? "
And list the hollow, " Beggared, lost—all ruined,
   poor and lost ! "

" Nay, say not so, for I am here to share misfortune's hour,
And prove how better far than gold is love's un-
   failing dower.
Let wealth take wings and fly away, as far as
   wings can soar,
The bird of love will hover near, and only sing the
   more."

' All lost, papa ? Why, here am I ; and, father, see
   how tall;
I measure fully three feet four upon the kitchen
   wall;
I'll tend the flowers, feed the birds, and have such
   lots of fun,
I'm big enough to work, papa, for I'm the oldest
   son."

" And I, papa, am almost five," says curly-headed
   Rose,
" And I can learn to sew, papa, and make all
   dolly's clothes.
But what *is* ' poor '—to stay at home, and have no
   place to go ?
Oh! then I'll ask the Lord, to-night, to make us
   always so."

" I'se here, papa; I isn't lost! " and on his father's
   knee
He lays his sunny head to rest, that baby-boy of
   three.
" And if you get too poor to live," says little Rose,
   " you know
There is a better place, papa, a heaven where we
   can go.

" And God will come and take us there, dear
   father, if we pray;
We needn't fear the road, papa, He surely knows
   the way."
Then from the corner, staff in hand, the grandma
   rises slow,
Her snowy cap-strings in the breeze soft fluttering to and fro;

Totters across the parlor floor, by aid of kindly
   hands,
Counting in every little face, her life's declining
   sands ;
Reaches his side, and whispers low, "God's prom-
   ises are sure ;
For every grievous wound, my son, He sends a
   ready cure."

The father clasps her hand in his, and quickly
   turns aside,
The heaving chest, the rising sigh, the coming
   tear, to hide;
Folds to his heart those loving ones, and kisses
   o'er and o'er
That noble wife whose faithful heart he little
   knew before.

" May God forgive me! What is wealth to these
   more precious things,
Whose rich affection round my heart a ceaseless
   odor flings ?
I think He knew my sordid soul was getting proud
   and cold,
And thus to save me, gave me *these*, and took
   away my *gold*.

" Dear ones, forgive me ; nevermore will I forget
   the rod
That brought me safely unto you, and led me back
   to God,
I am not poor while these bright links of precious
   love remain,
And, Heaven helping, nevermore shall blindness
   hide the chain."

                  —*Cora M. Eager.*

FARMER GREEN.

A QUIET house, just off the road,
Of plenteous peace the sweet abode ;
The roses climbed about the door,
The porch with eglantine ran o'er,
While 'neath its purple flowers there sat
A jolly fellow, sleek and fat,
The master of the thriving farm,
Whose thrifty head and stalwart arm
Had pleased old Mother Earth so well
She made his barns and bins to swell
With all the fatness of the land,
Bestowed from out her generous hand.
Along the sun-beat, dusty road
A one-legged jaded soldier strode.
He stopped and viewed the quiet scene,
In contrast with the place he'd been ;
Then, humbly, to the porch he walked,
And to the prosperous farmer talked :
" My friend, I was a soldier when
My country called for willing men,
I lost my leg, the story's told ;
I have not thriven as of old."
" After my long and weary trudge,
A bit of bread you'll not begrudge ? "
The farmer scanned from top to toe
His form ; then bluntly answered " No! "
The soldier felt his bosom swell,
And said : " A drink from out this well
Will quench my thirst ; by Heaven it's sent,
And costs you not a single cent."
But still the farmer, like a foe,
Answered the soldier, gruffly, " No! "
" Good sir," the soldier humbly plead,
" I'm weary, footsore—almost dead.
A storm it comes, not far away ;
Within your barn, pray, let me stay."
But still the farmer frowned and said :
" My barn's no place to make a bed."
The soldier, now, with flashing eyes,
And stick upraised, in anger cries,

" You ill-bred, ill-fed man of greed,
I stood your friend in hour of need,
I risked my life that you might live
Amid the plenty peace can give.
And now from out your plenteous store
You'd grudge me bread and drink, or straw
Whereon to lay my weary head.
You grudge me ground, if I were dead,
To hide me from your stingy eye.
Keep what you've got, and so good-by ! "
The farmer laughed, and as he rose,
Kept still repeating many No's!
" What is your name ? John Brown ; 'tis good,
Now, Brown, I'll ask you what you would
Have thought of me if, with good meat,
Fresh eggs, fat pullets, bacon sweet,
I'd brought you out a bit of bread,
And, when you asked for water, said
That you might drink from yonder tin,
When I've good cider here within ?
D'ye think I'd let you sleep on straw
When I've got beds on every floor ?
Come in my house and I'll forget,
While paying off our little debt,
That you supposed old Farmer Green
Could be so dreadful close and mean
As to grudge a bite, a drink and bed,
While he so bountifully is fed.
No! No! my brave, I never sin,
Knowing it such, and so, come in ! "
       —J. W. Watson.

ANNIE'S TICKET.

PLEASE, sir, I have brought you the ticket
 You gave her a short week ago—
My own little girl I am meaning,
 The one with the fair hair, you know,
And the blue eyes so gentle and tender,
 And sweet as the angels above.
God help me, she's one of them now, sir,
 And I've nothin' at all left to love.

It came on me sudden, ye see, sir ;
 She was never an ailin' child,
Though her face was as white as a lily
 And her ways just that quiet and mild.
The others was always a trouble,
 And botherin', too, every way,
But the first tears that ever she cost me
 Are them that I'm sheddin' to-day.

'Twas on Tuesday night that she sickened,
 She'd been blithe as a bird all day,
Wid the ticket ye gave her,
 And never another word
But " Mammie, just think of the music,"
 And, " Mammie, they'll give us ice-cream.
We can roll on the turf and pick posies;
 O Mammie! it's just like a dream! "

And so, when the fever came on her,
 It seemed the one thought in her brain.
'Twould have melted the heart in your breast
 To hear her, again and again,
Beggin', " Mammie, oh! plaze get me ready,
 The boat will be goin' off, I say,
I hear the bell ring. Where's me ticket ?
 Oh! won't we be happy to-day ! "

Three days she raved with the fever,
 Wid her face and her hands in a flame,
But on Friday at noon she grew quiet,
 She knew me, and called me by name.
My heart gave a leap when I heard it,
 But, O sir! it turned me to stone,
The look on the face, pinched and drawn like,
 I knew God had sent for His own.

And she knew it too, sir, the creature,
 And said, when I told her the day,
In her weak little voice," Mammie, darlin',
 Don't cry 'cause I'm goin away.
To-morrow they'll go to the picnic—
 They'll have beautiful times, I know,
But Heaven is like it, and better,
 And so I am ready to go.

" And Mammie, I ain't a bit frightened,
 There's many a little girl died,
And it seems like the dear lovin' Saviour
 Was standin' right here by me side
Take my ticket, dear Mammie, and ask them
 If some other child, poor and sick,
That hasn't got Heaven and Jesus,
 May go in my place and be glad."

And then, with " Good-bye, Mammie darlin',"
 She drew my lips down to her own,
And the One she had felt close beside her
 Bent too, and I sat there alone,
And so I have brought you the ticket,
 Though me heart seems ready to break,
To ask you to let some poor creature
 Feel glad for my dead darlin's sake.

WAITING FOR THE MAIL.

WITH anxious features worn and pale,
 He waits the coming of the mail;
Each day he asks, with hope and fear,
 " My letter, is my letter here ?"
Each day he hears in silence dumb;
 " Not yet, old man, it has not come."
The harmless madman, old and gray,
 No one would jeer or drive away.
" Ah me," he says, " long years have past,
 But it will come, 'twill come at last."
And so he waits in silence dumb,
 The letter that will never come.

Through misty vision of his tears,
 He sees the long, far-sundered years,
The past comes up before him there,
 When he was strong and she was fair.
Once more he feels in very truth,
 The leaping pulses of his youth;
A strong, strange joy he feels again
 The old wild fever in his brain ;
An angry word, a careless tone,
 And she has gone and he's alone.
Since then he waits in silence dumb,
 The letter that will never come.

Alas! his poor old wits are fled,
 He cannot know, that she is dead ;
And so he asks it, o'er and o'er.
 The same old question as before.
He wakes with morning light to say:
 " My letter, it will come to-day.'
With tottering limbs that almost fail,
 He creeps each morning to the mail,
And hears with ever new regret,
 " Not yet, old man, not yet, not yet."
And so he waits in silence dumb,
 The letter that will never come.

Ah, me! poor madman, even we
 Are dupes of fickle destiny ;
In ceaseless hope we waiting sit,
 For missives that were never writ.
We wait to see the harvest grown,
 Of seed that we have never sown;
We seek the harbor mouth to hail
 The vessels that will never sail.
We wait to see our garner filled
 With fruits of fields we have not tilled.
We wait in gathering stillness dumb,
 For letters that will never come.
       —S. W. Foss.

THE CLOWN'S BABY.

It was out on the Western frontier—
　The miners rugged and brown,
Were gathered around the posters;
　The circus had come to town!
The great tent shone in the darkness,
　Like a wonderful palace of light.
And rough men crowded the entrance—
　Shows didn't come every night!

Not a woman's face among them;
　Many a face that was bad,
And some that were only vacant,
　And some that were very sad.
And behind a canvas curtain,
　In a corner of the place,
The clown, with chalk and vermillion,
　Was "making up" his face.

A weary-looking woman,
　With a smile that still was sweet,
Sewed on a little garment,
　With a cradle at her feet.
Pantaloon stood ready and waiting,
　It was the time for the going on;
But the clown in vain searched wildly—
　The "property baby" was gone.

He murmured, impatiently hunting,
　"It's strange that I cannot find—
There! I've looked in every corner;
　It must have been left behind!"
The miners were stamping and shouting,
　They were not patient men;
The clown bent over the cradle—
　"I must take *you*, little Ben!"

The mother started and shivered,
　But trouble and want were near;
She lifted her baby gently:
　"You'll be very careful, dear?"
"Careful? You foolish darling"—
　How tenderly it was said!
What a smile shone thro' the chalk and paint—
　"I love each hair on his head!"

The noise rose into an uproar,
　Misrule for the time was king;
The clown with a foolish chuckle,
　Bolted into the ring.
But as, with a squeak and flourish,
　The fiddles closed the'r tune,
"You'll hold him as if he were made of glass?"
　Said the clown to pantaloon.

The jovial fellow nodded;
　"I've a couple myself," he said,
"I know how to handle 'em, bless you!
　Old fellow, go ahead!"
The fun grew fast and furious.
　And not one of all the crowd
Had guessed that the baby was alive,
　When he suddenly laughed aloud.

Oh, that baby laugh! it was echoed
　From the benches with a ring,
And the roughest customer there sprang up
　With "Boys, it's the real thing!"
The ring was jammed in a minute,
　Not a man that did not strive
For "a shot at holding the baby"—
　The baby that was "alive!"

He was thronged by kneeling suitors
　In the midst of the dusty ring,
And he held his court right royally—
　The fair little baby king—

Till one of the shouting courtiers,
　A man with a bold, hard face,
The talk, for miles of the country,
　And the terror of the place,

Raised the little king to his shoulder,
　And chuckled "Look at that!"
As the chubby fingers clutched his hair,
　Then, "Boy's, hand round the hat!"
There never was such a hatful
　Of silver, and gold, and notes;
People are not always penniless
　Because they don't wear coats!

And then, "Three cheers for the baby!"
　I tell you those cheers were meant,
And the way in which they were given
　Was enough to raise the tent.
And then there was a sudden silence,
　And a gruff old miner said.
"Come, boys, enough of this rumpus!
　It's time it was put to bed."

So, looking a little sheepish,
　But with faces strangely bright,
The audience, somewhat lingering,
　Flocked out into the night.
And the bold-faced leader chuckled,
　"He wasn't a bit afraid!
He's as game as he is good-looking—
　Boys, that was a show that *paid*."
　　—*Margaret Vandergrift, in St. Nicholas,*

THE COUNTERSIGN WAS "MARY."

'Twas near the break of day, but still
　The moon was shining brightly;
The west wind as it passed the flowers
　Set each one swaying lightly;
The sentry slow paced to and fro
　A faithful night-watch keeping,
While in the tents behind him stretched,
　His comrades all were sleeping.

Slow to and fro the sentry paced,
　His musket on his shoulder,
But not a thought of death or war
　Was with the brave young soldier.
'Ah, ho! his heart was far away
　Where, on a western prairie,
A rose-twined cottage stood. That night
　The countersign was "Mary."

And there his own true love he saw,
　Her blue eyes kindly beaming;
Above them, on her sun-kissed brow,
　Her curls like sunlight gleaming,
And heard her singing, as she churned
　The butter in the dairy,
The song he loved the best. That night
　The countersign was "Mary."

"Oh, for one kiss from her!" he sighed,
　When up the lone road glancing,
He spied a form, a little form,
　With faltering steps advancing,
And as it neared him silently
　He gazed at it in wonder;
Then dropped his musket to his hand,
　And challenged: "Who goes yonder?"

Still on it came. "Not one step more,
　Be you man, or child, or fairy,
Unless you give the countersign,
　Halt! Who goes there?" "'Tis Mary,"

A sweet voice cried, and in his arms
The girl he'd left behind him
Half-fainting fell. O'er many miles
She'd bravely toiled to find him.

"I heard that you were wounded, dear,"
She sobbed: "my heart was breaking;
I could not stay a moment, but,
All other ties forsaken,
I travelled, by my grief made strong,
Kind heaven watching o'er me,
Until—unhurt and well?" "Yes, love,'
"At last you stood before me."

"They told me that I could not pass
The lines to seek my lover
Before day fairly came; but I
Pressed on ere night was over,
And as I told my name, I found
The way free as our prairie."
"Because, thank God! to-night," he said,
"The countersign is 'Mary.'"
—*Margaret Eytinge.*

THE GAMBLER'S WIFE.

DARK is the night! how dark! no light! no fire!
Cold on the hearth the last faint sparks expire!
Shivering she watches by the cradle side
For him who pledged her love—last year a bride!
"Hark! 'tis his footstep! No—'tis past; 'tis gone;
Tick!—tick! How wearily the time crawls on,
Why should he leave me thus? He once was kind,
And I believed 'twould last—how mad! how blind!
Rest thee, my babe—rest on! 'tis hunger's cry!
Sleep, for there is no food, the fount is dry.
Famine and cold their wearying work have done;
My heart must break! And thou!"—the clock strikes one.
"Hush! 'tis the dice-box. Yes, he's there, he's there!
For this, for this, he leaves me to despair!
Leaves love, leaves truth, his wife, his child—for what?
The wanton's smile—the villain—and the sot!
Yet I'll not curse him; no—'tis all in vain.
'Tis long to wait, but sure he'll come again;
And I could starve and bless him, but for you,
My child—*his* child—oh, fiend!"—The clock strikes two.
"Hark! how the sign-board creaks, the blast howls by!
Moan—moan! A dirge swells through the cloudy sky!
Ha! 'tis his knock—he comes—he comes home once more—
'Tis but the lattice flaps. Thy hope is o'er.
Can he desert me thus? He knows I stay
Night after night in loneliness to pray
For his return—and yet he sees no tear.
No, no! it cannot be. He will be here.
Nestle more closely, dear one, to my heart
Thou'rt cold—thou'rt freezing; but we will not part.
Husband, I die! Father, it is not he!
Oh, Heaven, protect my child!"—The clock strikes three.
They're gone! they're gone! The glimmering spark hath fled.
The wife and child are number'd with the dead!
On the cold hearth, outstretched in solemn rest,
The child lies frozen on its mother's breast!
The gambler came at last—but all was o'er—
Dead silence reigned around—he groaned—he spoke no more!
—*Coates*

WHICH SHALL IT BE!

WHICH shall it be? Which shall it be?
I looked at John, John looked at me,
And when I found that I must speak,
My voice seemed strangely low and weak.
"Tell me again what Robert said;"
And then I listening bent my head—
     This is his letter:

     "I will give
A house and land while you shall live,
If, in return, from out your seven,
One child to me for aye is given."

I looked at John's old garments worn;
I thought of all that he had borne
Of poverty, and work, and care,
Which I, though willing, could not share;
I thought of seven young mouths to feed,
Of seven little children's need,
     And then of this.

     "Come, John," said I.
"We'll choose among them as they lie
Asleep." So, walking hand in hand,
Dear John and I surveyed our band;
First to the cradle lightly stepped,
Where Lilian, the baby, slept.
Softly the father stooped to lay
His rough hand down in loving way,
When dream or whisper made her stir,
And huskily he said: "Not her!"

We stooped beside the trundle bed,
And one long ray of twilight shed
Athwart the boyish faces there,
In sleep so beautiful and fair;
I saw on James's rough red cheek
A tear undried. E'er John could speak,
"He's but a baby, too," said I,
And kissed him as we hurried by.
Pale, patient Robbie's angel face
Still in sleep bore suffering's trace,
"No, for a thousand crowns, not him!"
He whispered, while our eyes were dim.

Poor Dick! bad Dick! our wayward son—
Turbulent, restless, idle one—
Could he be spared? Nay, He who gave
Bade us befriend him to the grave;
Only a mother's heart could be
Patient enough for such as he;
"And so," said John, "I would not dare
To take him from her bedside prayer."

Then stole we softly up above,
And knelt by Mary, child of love;
"Perhaps for her 'twould better be,
I said to John. Quite silently
He lifted up a curl that lay
Across her cheek in wilful way,
And shook his head: "Nay, love, not thee,"
The while my heart beat audibly.

Only one more, our eldest lad,
Trusty and truthful, good and glad,
So like his father. "No, John, no!
I cannot, will not, let him go."
And so we wrote in courteous way,
We could not give one child away;
And afterward toil lighter seemed,
Thinking of that of which we dreamed;
Happy in truth that not one face
Was missed from its accustomed place;
Thankful to work for all the seven,
Trusting the rest to One in heaven.

THE COLLIER'S DYING CHILD

THE cottage was a thatched one, its outside old
 and mean;
Yet everything within that cot was wondrous neat
 and clean:
The night was dark and stormy—the wind was
 blowing wild;—
A patient mother sat beside the deathbed of her
 child—
A little, worn-out creature—his once bright eyes
 grown dim;
It was a Collier's child—they called him "Little
 Jim."
And oh! to see the briny tears fast flowing down
 her cheek,
As she offered up a prayer in thought!—she was
 afraid to speak,
Lest she might waken one she loved far dearer
 than her life:
For she had all a mother's heart, that wretched
 collier's wife.
With hands uplifted, see, she kneels beside the
 sufferer's bed,
And prays that God shall spare her boy, and take
 herself instead:
She gets her answer from her child—soft falls
 these words from him—
"Mother! the angels do so smile, and beckon little Jim!
I have no pain, dear mother, now; but, oh! I am
 so dry:
Just moisten poor Jim's lips once more; and,
 mother, do not cry!"
With gentle, trembling haste, she held a tea-cup
 to his lips—
He smiled to thank her—then he took three little
 tiny sips.
"Tell father, when he comes from work, I said
 'good night!' to him;
And, mother, now I'll go to sleep." . . . . Alas!
 poor Little Jim!
She saw that he was dying! the child she loved so
 dear,
Had utter'd the last words she'd ever wish to
 hear.
The cottage door is opened—the Collier's step is
 heard;
The father and the mother meet, but neither speak
 a word:
He felt that all was over—he knew the child was
 dead!
He took the candle in his hand, and stood beside
 the bed:
His quivering lip gave token of the grief he'd fain
 conceal;
And see, the mother joins him!—the stricken
 couple kneel;
With hearts bowed down by sorrow, they humbly
 ask, of him
In heaven, once more that they may meet their
 own poor "Little Jim!"

      —*Farmer.*

"NOBODY'S CHILD."

Alone in the dreary, pitiless street,
Wity my torn old dress and bare cold feet,
All day I have wandered to and fro,
Hungry and shivering, and nowhere to go;
The night's coming on in darkness and dread,
And the chill sleet beating upon my bare head.
Oh! why does the wind blow on me so wild?
Is it because I am nobody's child?

Just over the way there's a flood of light,
And warmth and beauty and all things bright;
Beautiful children, in robes so fair,
Are caroling songs in rapture there.

I wonder if they in their blissful glee,
Would pity a poor little beggar like me,
Wandering alone in the merciless street,
Naked and shivering and nothing to eat

Oh! what shall I do when the night comes down,
In its terrible blackness all over the town?
Shall lay me down 'neath the angry sky,
On the cold, hard pavement, alone to die,
When the beautiful children their prayers have
 said,
And their mammas have tucked them up snugly
 in bed?
For no dear mamma on me ever smiled—
Why is it, I wonder, I'm nobody's child!

No father, no mother, no sister, not one
In all the world loves, e'en the little dogs run
When I wander too near; 'tis wondrous to see
How everything shrinks from a beggar like me!
Perhaps 'tis a dream; but sometimes when I lie
Gazing far up in the deep, blue sky,
Watching for hours some large, bright star,
I fancy the beautiful gates are ajar.

And a host of white-robed nameless things,
Come fluttering o'er me on gilded wings;
A hand that is strangely soft and fair
Caresses gently my tangled hair,
And a voice like the carol of some wild bird—
The sweetest voice that was ever heard—
Calls me many a dear pet name,
Till my heart and spirit are all aflame.

They tell me of such unbounded love,
And bid me come up to their home above;
And then with such pitiful, sad surprise,
The look at me with their sweet, tender eyes,
And it seems to me, out of the dreary night,
I am going up to that world of light;
And away from the hunger and storm so wild,
I am sure I shall then be somebody's child.

THE DIAMOND WEDDING.

COME, sit close by my side, my darling,
 Sit up very close to-night;
Let me clasp your tremulous fingers
 In mine, as tremulous, quite;
Lay your silvery head on my bosom,
 As you did when 'twas shining gold;
Somehow I know no difference,
 Though they say we are very old.

'Tis seventy-five years ago, to-night, wife,
 Since we knelt at the alter low,
And the fair young minister of God
 (He died long years ago,)
Pronounced us one, that Christmas eve—
 How short they've seemed to me,
The years—and yet, I'm ninety-seven,
 And you are ninety-three.

That night I placed on your finger
 A band of purest gold;
And to-night I see it shining
 On the withered hand I hold,
How it lightens up the memories
 That o'er my vision come!
First of all are the merry children
 That once made glad our home.

There was Benny, our darling Benny,
 Our first-born pledge of bliss,
As beautiful a boy as ever
 Felt a mother's loving kiss.
'Twas hard—as we watched him fading
 Like a floweret day by day—
To feel that He who had lent him
 Was calling him away.

My heart it grew very bitter
As I bowed beneath the stroke;
And yours, though you said so little,
I knew was almost broke.
We made him a grave 'neath the daisies
(There are five now, instead of one),
And we have learned when our Father chastens
To say, "Thy will be done."

Then came Lillie and Allie—twin cherubs
Just spared from the courts of heaven
To comfort our hearts for a moment;
God took as soon as he'd given.
Then Katie, our gentle Katie!
We thought her very fair,
With her blue eyes soft and tender,
And her curls of auburn hair.

Like a queen she looked at her bridal
(I thought it were you instead);
But her ashen lips kissed her first-born,
And mother and child were dead.
We said that of all our number
We had two, our pride and stay—
Two noble boys, Fred and Harry;— .
But God thought the other way.

Far away on the plains of Shiloh,
Fred sleeps in an unknown grave:
With his ship and noble sailors,
Harry sank beneath the wave,
So sit closer, darling, closer—
Let me clasp your hand in mine:
Alone we commenced life's journey,
Alone we are left behind.

Your hair, once gold, to silver
They say by age has grown,
But I know it has caught its whiteness
From the halo round His throne.
They gave us a diamond wedding
This Christmas eve, dear wife;
But I know your orange-blossoms
Will be a crown of life.

'Tis dark; the lamps should be lighted;
And your hand has grown so cold.
Has the fire gone out? How I shiver!
But, then, we are very old.
Hush! I hear sweet strains of music:
Perhaps the guests have come.
No—'tis the children's voices—
I know them, every one.

*   *   *   *   *

On that Christmas eve they found them—
Her hand in his still rests;
But they never knew their children
Had been their wedding guests.
With her head upon his bosom,
That had never ceased its love,
They held their diamond wedding
In the mansion house above.

THE OLD FORSAKEN SCHOOL-HOUSE.

THEY'VE left the school-house, Charley, where
years ago we sat.
And shot our paper bullets at the master's time-
worn hat;
The hook is gone on which it hung, and the master sleepeth now
Where school-boy tricks can never cast a shadow
o'er his brow.

They've built a new, imposing one—the pride of
all the town,
And laughing lads and lasses go its broad steps
up and down;
A tower crowns its summit with a new, a monster
bell,
That youthful ears, in distant homes, may hear its
music swell.

I'm sitting in the old one, with its battered, hinge-
less door;
The windows are all broken, and the stones lie on
floor;
I, alone, of all the boys who romped and studied
here,
Remain to see it battered up and left so lone and
drear.

I'm sitting on the same old bench where we sat
side by side
And carved our names upon the desk, when not
by master eyed;
Since then *a dozen* boys have sought their great
skill to display,
And, like the foot-prints on the sand, *our* names
have passed away.

'Twas here we learned to conjugate "amo, amas,
amat,"
While glances from the lasses made our heart go
pit-a-pat;
'Twas here we fell in love, you know, with girls
who looked us through—
Yours with her piercing eyes of black, and *mine*
with eyes of blue.

Our sweethearts—pretty girls were they—to us
how very dear—
Bow down your head with me, my boy, and shed
for them a tear;
With them the earthly school is out; each lovely
maid now stands
Before the one Great Master, in the "house not
made with hands."

You tell me you are far out West; a lawyer, deep
in laws,
With Joe, who sat behind us here, and tickled us
with straws;
Look out for number one, my boys; may wealth
come at your touch;
But with your long, strong legal straws don't
tickle men too much.

Here, to the right, sat Jimmy Jones—you must remember Jim—
He's teaching now, and punishing, as master pun-
ished him;
What an unlucky lad he was? his sky was dark
with woes;
Whoever did the *sinning* it was Jim who got the
blows.

Those days are all gone by, my boys; life's hill
we're going down,
With here and there a silver hair amid the
school-boy brown;
But memory can never die, so we'll talk o'er the
joys
We shared together, in this house, when you and I
were boys.

Though ruthless hands may tear it down—this old
house lone and drear,
They'll not destroy the characters that started
out from here;
Time's angry waves may sweep the shore and
wash out all beside;
Bright as the stars that shine above, *they* shall
for aye abide.

I've seen the new house, Charley; 'tis the pride
of all the town,
And laughing lads and lasses go its broad steps
up and down:
But you or I, my dear old friend, can't love it half
as well
As this condemned, forsaken one, with cracked
and tongueless bell.
—John H. Yates.

AN OLD SWEETHEART OF MINE.

As one who cons at evening o'er an album all
alone,
And muses on the faces of the friends that he has
known:
So I turn the leaves of fancy till in shadowy de-
sign
I find the smiling features of an old sweetheart of
mine.

The lamplight seems to glimmer with a flicker of
surprise
As I turn it low to rest me of the dazzle in my
eyes,
And light my pipe in silence, save a sigh that
seems to yoke
Its fate with my tobacco, and to vanish in the
smoke.

'Tis a fragrant retrospection, for the loving
thoughts that start
Into being are like perfumes from the blossoms of
the heart;
And to dream the old dreams over is a luxury di-
vine,
When my truant fancy wanders with that old
sweetheart of mine.

Though, I hear, beneath my study, like a fluttering of wings,
The voices of my children and the mother as she
sings,
I feel no twinge of conscience to deny me any
theme
When care has cast her anchor in the harbor of a
dream.

In fact, to speak in earnest, I believe it adds a
charm
To spice the good a trifle with a little dust of
harm;
For I find an extra flavor in memory's mellow
vine
That makes me drink the deeper to that old sweetheart of mine.

A face of lily beauty and a form of airy grace
Floats out of my tobacco as the genius from the
vase;
And I thrill beneath the glances of a pair of azure
eyes
As glowing as the summer and as tender as the
skies.

I can see the pink sun-bonnet and the little checkered dress
She wore when first I kissed her, and she answered the caress
With the written declaration that "as surely as
the vine
Grew 'round the stump, she loved me," that old
sweetheart of mine.

And again I feel the pressure of her slender little
hand
As we used to talk together of the future we had
planned;
When I should be a poet, and with nothing else to
do
But to write the tender verses that she set the
music to.

When we should live together in a cosy little cot
Hid in a nest of roses, with a tiny garden spot
Where the vines were ever fruitful and the
weather ever fine,
And the birds were ever singing for that old
sweetheart of mine.

When I should be her lover forever and a day,
And she my faithful sweetheart till the golden
hair was gray:
And we should be so happy that when either's lips
were dumb
They should not smile in heaven till the other's
kiss had come.

But, ah, my dream is broken by a step upon the
stair.
And the door is softly opened, and my wife is
standing there;
Yet with eagerness and rapture all my visions I
resign
To meet the living presence of that old sweetheart
of mine.

—*James Whitcomb Riley.*

IN THE MINING TOWN.

" 'Tis the last time, darling," he gently said,
As he kissed her lips like the cherries red.
While a fond look shone in his eyes of brown!
" My own is the prettiest girl in town!
To-morrow the bells from the tower will ring
A joyful peal. Was there ever a king
So truly blest, on his royal throne,
As I shall be when I claim my own?"

'Twas a fond farewell; 'twas a sweet good-by,
But she watched him go with a troubled sigh.
So, into the basket that swayed and swung
O'er the yawning abyss, he lightly sprung.
And the joy of her heart seemed turned to woe
As they lowered him to the depths below.
Her sweet, young face, with its tresses brown,
Was the fairest face in the mining town.

Lo! the morning came; but the marriage bell,
High up in the tower, rang a mournful knell
For the true heart buried 'neath earth and stone,
Far down in the heart of the mine—alone.
A sorrowful peal on their wedding-day,
For the breaking heart and the heart of clay;
And the face that looked from her tresses brown,
Was the saddest face in the mining town.

Thus time rolled along on its weary way,
Until fifty years, with their shadows gray,
Had darkened the light of her sweet eyes' glow,
And had turned the brown of her hair to snow.
Oh! never the kiss from a husband's lips,
Or the clasp of a child's sweet finger tips,
Had lifted one moment the shadows brown
From the saddest heart in the mining town.

Far down in the depths of the mine, one day,
In the loosened earth they were digging away;
They discovered a face, so young, so fair;
From the smiling lip to the bright brown hair,
Untouched by the fingers of Time's decay;
When they drew him up to the light of day,
The wondering people gathered 'round
To gaze at a man thus strangely found.

Then a woman came from among the crowd,
With her long white hair and her slight form
bowed.
She silently knelt by the form of clay,
And kissed the lips that were cold and gray.
Then, the sad old face, with its snowy hair
On his youthful bosom lay pillowed there,
He had found her at last, his waiting bride,
And the people buried them side by side.

—*Rose Hartwick Thorpe.*

. THE TELEGRAM.

" Is this the tel'graph office ? "
  Asked a childish voice one day,
As I noted the click of my instrument
  With its message from far away ,
As it ceased, I turned ; at my elbow
  Stood the merest scrap of a boy,
Whose childish face was all aglow
  With the light of hidden joy.

The golden curls on his forehead
  Shaded eyes of deepest blue,
As if a bit of the summer sky
  Had lost in them its hue ;
They scanned my office rapidly
  From ceiling down to floor,
Then turned on mine their eager gaze,
  As he asked the question o'er.

" Is this the tel'graph office ? "
  " It is, my little man,"
I said, " pray tell me what you want,
  And I'll help you if I can ; "
Then the blue eyes grew more eager,
  And the breath came thick and fast ;
And I saw within the chubby hands,
  A folded paper grasped.

" Nurse told me," he said, " that the lightning
  Came down on the wires some day ;
And my mamma has gone to heaven
  And I'm lonely since she is away,
For my papa is very busy
  And hasn't much time for me,
So I thought I'd write her a letter,
  And I've brought it for you to see

" I've printed it big so the angels
  Could read out quick the name,
And carry it straight to my mamma,
  And tell her how it came ;
And now won't you please to take it,
  And throw it up good and strong,
Against the wires in a funder shower,
  And the angels will take it along."

Ah ! what could I tell the darling ?
  For my eyes were filling fast ;
I turned away to hide the tears,
  But I cheerfully spoke at last :
" I'll do the best I can, my child,"
  'Twas all that I could say ;
" Thank you," he said, then scanned the sky ;
  " Do you think it will funder to-day ? "

But the blue sky smiled in answer,
  And the sun shone dazzling bright,
And his face, as he slowly turned away,
  Lost some of its gladsome light ;
" But nurse," he said, " if I stay so long,
  Won't let me come any more :
So good-bye, I'll come and see you again
  Right after a funder shower."

HOW THE PARSON BROKE THE SABBATH.

On the grave of Parson Williams
  The grass is brown and bleached ;
It is the more than fifty winters
  Since he lived and laughed and preached.

But his memory in New England
  No winter snows can kill ;
Of his goodness and his drollness
  Countless legends linger still.

And among those treasured legends,
  I hold this one as a boon—
How he got in Deacon Crosby's hay
  On a Sunday afternoon.

He was midway in a sermon,
  Most orthodox, on grace,
When a sound of distant thunder
  Broke the quiet of the place.

Now the meadow of the Crosby's
  Lay full within his sight,
As he glanced from out the window
  Which stood open on his right.

And the green and fragrant haycocks
  By acres there did stand !
Not a meadow like the deacon's
  Far or near in all the land.

Quick and loud the claps of thunder
  Went rolling to the skies,
And the parson saw his deacon
  Looking out with anxious eyes.

" Now, my brethren," called the parson,
  And he called with might and main,
" We must get in Brother Crosby's hay ;
  'Tis our duty now most plain ! "

And he shut the great red Bible,
  And tossed his sermon down ;
Not a man could turn more swiftly
  Than the parson in that town.

And he ran now to the meadow,
  With all his strength and speed ;
And the congregation followed,
  All bewildered in his lead.

With a will they worked and shouted,
  And cleared the fields apace ;
And the parson led the singing,
  While the sweat rolled down his face.

And it thundered fiercer, louder,
  And the dark grew east and west ;
But the hay was under cover,
  And the parson had worked best.

And again in pew and pulpit
  Their places took, composed ;
And the parson preached his sermon
  To "fifteenth," where it closed.

                 —H. H.

OLD AUNT MARY'S.

Wasn't it pleasant, oh, brother mine,
In those old days of the lost sunshine
Of youth, when the Saturday's chores were
  — through,
And the " Sunday wood " in the kitchen, too,
And we went visiting, " me and you,"
  Out to old Aunt Mary's ?

It all comes back so clear to-day !
Though I am as bald as you are gray—
Out by the barn-lot and down by the lane
We patter along in the dust again
As light as the tips of the drops of the rain,
  Out to old Aunt Mary's !

We cross the pasture and through the wood
Where the old gray snag of the poplar stood;
Where the hammering "red-heads" hopped awry,
And the buzzard "raised" in the "clearing"
   sky.
And lolled and circled as we went by,
   Out to old Aunt Mary's.

And then in the dust of the road again:
And the teams we met, and the countrymen;
And the long highway with sunshine spread
As thick as butter on country bread,
Our cares behind and our hearts ahead,
   Out to old Aunt Mary's.

Why, I see her now in the open door
Where the gourds grew up the sides, and o'er
The clapboard roof! And her face—ah, me,
Wasn't it good for a boy to see,
And wasn't it good for a boy to be
   Out to old Aunt Mary's!

And, oh, my brother, so far away,
This is to tell you she waits to-day
To welcome us. Aunt Mary fell
Asleep this morning, whispering, "Tell
The boys to come!" and all is well
   Out to old Aunt Mary's!
        —*James Whitcomb Riley.*

GUILTY OR NOT GUILTY.

She stood at the bar of justice,
   A creature wan and wild,
In form too small for a woman,
   In features too old for a child,
For a look so worn and pathetic
   Was stamped on her pale young face,
It seemed long years of suffering
   Must have left that silent trace.

"Your name," said the judge, as he eyed her
   With kindly look yet keen,
"Is Mary McGuire, if you please, sir.
   "And your age?"—"I am turned fifteen."
"Well, Mary," and then from a paper
   He slowly and gravely read,
"You are charged here—I'm sorry to say it—
   With stealing three loaves of bread.

"You look not like an offender,
   And I hope that you can show
The charge to be false. Now, tell me,
   Are you guilty of this, or no?"
A passionate burst of weeping
   Was at first her sole reply,
But she dried her eyes in a moment,
   And looked in the judge's eye.

"I will tell you just how it was, sir,
   My father and mother are dead,
And my little brother and sisters
   Were hungry and asked me for bread.
At first I earned it for them
   By working hard all day,
But somehow times were bad, sir,
   And the work all fell away.

"I could get no more employment
   The weather was bitter cold,
The young ones cried and shivered—
   (Little Johnny's but four years old)—
So, what was I to do, sir?
   I am guilty, but do not condemn,
I *took*—oh, was it *stealing?*—
   The bread to give to them."

Every man in the court room—
   Gray-beard and thoughtless youth—
Knew, as he looked upon her,
   That the prisoner spake the truth,
Out from their pockets came kerchiefs,
   Out from their eyes sprung tears,
And out from their old faded wallets
   Treasures hoarded for years.

The judge's face was a study—
   The strangest you ever saw,
As he cleared his throat and murmured
   Something about the *law.*
For one so learned in such matters,
   So wise in dealing with men,
He seemed, on a simple question,
   Sorely puzzled just then.

But no one blamed him or wondered,
   When at last these words they heard.
"The sentence of this young prisoner
   Is, for the present, deferred."
And no one blamed him or wondered
   When he went to her and smiled,
And tenderly led from the court-room,
   Himself, the "guilty" child.

THE LOST KISS.

I put by the half-written poem,
   While the pen, idly trailed in my hand,
Writes on: "Had I words to complete it,
   Who'd read it, or who'd understand?"
But the little bare feet on the stairway,
   And the faint, smothered laugh in the hall,
And the eerie-low lisp on the silence,
   Cry up to me over it all.

So I gathered it up—where was broken
   The tear-faded thread of my theme,
Telling how, as one night I sat writing,
   A fairy broke in on my dream;
A little inquisitive fairy—
   My own little girl, with the gold
Of the sun in her hair, and the dewy
   Blue eyes of the fairies of old.

'Twas the dear little girl I had scolded.
   "For was it a moment like this,"
I said, "when she knew I was busy,
   To come romping in for a kiss?
Come rowdying up from her mother,
   And clamoring there at my knee
For 'one 'little kiss for my dolly,
   And un 'ittle uzzer to me!'"

God pity the heart that repelled her
   And the cold hand that turned her away
And take from the lips that denied her
   This answerless prayer of to-day!
Take, Lord, from my mem'ry forever
   That pitiful sob of despair,
And the patter and trip of the little bare feet,
   And the one piercing cry on the stair!

I put by the half-written poem,
   While the pen, idly trailed in my hand,
Writes on: "Had I words to complete it,
   Who'd read it, or who'd understand?"
But the little bare feet on the stairway,
   And the faint, smothered laugh in the hall,
And the eerie-low lisp on the silence,
   Cry up to me over it all.
        —*James Whitcomb Riley.*

DRIVING HOME THE COWS.

OUT of the clover and blue-eyed grass,
 He turned them into the river-lane;
One after another he let them pass,
 And fastened the meadow bars again.

Under the willows and over the hill,
 He patiently followed their sober space;
The merry whistle for once was still,
 And something shadowed the sunny face.

Only a boy! and his father had said
 He never would let his youngest go;
Two already were lying dead,
 Under the feet of the trampling foe.

But after the evening work was done,
 And the frogs were loud in the meadow swamp,
Over his shoulder he slung his gun,
 And stealthily followed the foot-path damp.

Across the clover and through the wheat,
 With resolute heart and purpose grim,
Though cold was the dew on the hurrying feet,
 And the blind bats flitting startled him.

Thrice since then had the lane been white,
 And the orchard sweet with apple bloom;
And now when the cows came back at night,
 The feeble father drove them home.

For news had come to the lonely farm
 That three were lying where two had lain;
And the old man's tremulous palsied arm
 Could never lean on a son's again.

The summer day grew cold and late,
 He went for the cows when the work was done;
But down the lane, as he opened the gate,
 He saw them coming one by one.

Brindle, Ebony, Speckle, and Bess,
 Shaking their horns in the evening wind;
Cropping the buttercups out of the grass—
 But who was it following close behind?

Loosely swung in the idle air
 The empty sleeve of army blue;
And worn and pale, from the crisping hair,
 Looked out a face that the father knew.

For Southern prisons will sometimes yawn,
 And yield their dead unto life again;
And the day that comes with a cloudy dawn
 In golden glory at last may wane.

The great tears sprang to their meeting eyes;
 For the heart must speak when the lips are
  dumb;
And under the silent evening skies
 Together they followed the cattle home.

THE DRUNKARD'S WIFE.

LOUD roar the winds, the cutting ice-bolts fall,
 The whirling snow is borne along the air,
The frozen streams shriek to the wind's wild call—
 The pine trees writhe like giants in despair.

Cold by the hearth a shivering mother kneels,
 Clasped to her breast a hunger-dying child;
The life-blood in her veins with cold congeals—
 Starvation beams from out her dark eye wild.

"O God!" she cries, "O God, look on my child!
 Dear Heaven, have pity! my poor starling spare
To die—to die! those lips that on me smiled—
 To wither in the grave-mold this brow fair!

"Black gloom and darkness—chillier grows the
  night;
 The midnight bell has tolled; he is not here!
He lingers o'er the wine-cup red and bright—
 O God! O God! is morning drawing near?

"My babe—how cold; my tears freeze on thy
  cheek!
 O husband, come! why linger thus away?
Hark! hear the rushing of the wild winds bleak!
 No food—no fire to cheer the coming day!

"My loved, my lost, my husband, turn and flee!
 Oh, flee the monster, ere thy doom is fixed!
Cursed be the wine-cup! thrice accursed be he
 Who for his fellow-man hath poison mixed!

"My child, O mercy! pity from above!
 Why does he turn on me such wild, strange eyes?
Why does his face beam with such holy love?
 Ah, can it be he's waning to the skies!

"See how he gasps—he groans—O Death! O Death!
 My husband, come! he's dying—he our own!
Oh, for one kiss ere flees his blessed breath—
 Great God, 'tis o'er—and I am all alone!

"My darling one, my beautiful, my bright,
 Thou 'rt gone ere sorrow in thy breast was born;
I follow thee—flees far the pitchy night!
 Husband, farewell—O Saviour, breaks the morn!"

Wild the dark winds sang on; the drifting snow
 Wrapt the wan corpses in its pitying shroud.
The drunkard lingered in the wine's red glow,
 Where on the air fell laughter long and loud.

The eastern heavens blushed with waking life,
 The crimson day across the orient broke;
In lands where breezes with warm sweets are rife,
 The mother and her angel child awoke!
      —*Clara Augusta.*

SOMEBODY'S MOTHER.

THE woman was old and ragged and gray,
And bent with the chill of a winter's day;
The streets were white with a recent snow,
And the woman's feet with age were slow.

At the crowded crossing she waited long,
Jostled aside by the careless throng
Of human beings who passed her by,
Unheeding the glance of her anxious eye.

Down the street with laughter and shout,
Glad in the freedom of "school let out,"
Come happy boys, like a flock of sheep,
Hailing the snow piled white and deep;
Past the woman, so old and gray,
Hastened the children on their way.

None offered a helping hand to her,
So weak and timid, afraid to stir,
Lest the carriage wheels or the horses' feet
Should trample her down in the slippery street.

At last came out of the merry troop
The gayest boy of all the group;
He paused beside her, and whispered low,
"I'll help you across, if you wish to go."

Her aged hand on his strong young arm
She placed, and so without hurt or harm
He guided the trembling feet along,
Proud that his own were young and strong;
Then back again to his friends he went,
His young heart happy and well content.

"She's somebody's mother, boys, you know,
  For all she's aged, and poor and slow;
And some one, some time, may lend a hand
To help my mother—you understand ?—
If ever she's old and poor and gray,
And her own dear boy so far away."

"Somebody's mother " bowed low her head
In her home that night, and the prayer she said
Was: "God be kind to that noble boy,
Who is somebody's son and pride and joy."
Faint was the voice, and worn and weak,
But Heaven lists when its chosen speak ;
Angels caught the faltering word,
And "Somebody's Mother's " prayer was heard.

BILL MASON'S RIDE.

HALF an hour till train time, sir,
  An' a fearful dark time, too ;
Take a look at the switch-lights, Tom,
  Fetch in a stick when you're through.
"On time ? " well, yes, I guess so—
  Left the last station all right—
She'll come round the curve a flyin';
  Bill Mason comes up to-night.

You know Bill ? No! He's engineer,
  Been on the road all his life—
I'll never forget the mornin'
  He married his chuck of a wife,
'Twas the summer the mill hands struck—
  Just off work, every one ;
They kicked up a row in the village
  And killed old Donevan's son.

But hadn't been married mor'n an' hour,
  Up comes a message from Kress,
Orderin' Bill to go up there,
  And bring down the night express.
He left his gal in a hurry,
  And went up on number one,
Thinking of nothing but Mary,
  And the train he had to run.

And Mary sat down by the window
  To wait for the night express ;
And, sir, if she hadn't a' done so,
  She'd been a widow, I guess.
For it must a' been nigh midnight
  When the mill-hands left the Ridge—
They come down—the drunken devils!
  Tore up a rail from the bridge.
But Mary heard 'em a workin'
  And guessed there was somethin' wrong—
And in less than fifteen minutes,
  Bill's train it would be along!

She couldn't come here to tell *us*.
  A mile—It would'nt a done—
So she jest grabbed up a lantern,
  And made for the bridge alone.
Then down came the night express, sir,
  And Bill was makin' her climb!
But Mary held the lantern,
  A-swingin' it all the time.

Well! by Jove! Bill saw the signal,
  And he stopped the night express,
And he found his Mary cryin'
  On the track, in her weddin' dress;
Cryin' an laughin' for joy, sir,
  An' holdin' on to the light—
Hello! here's the train—good-bye, sir,
  Bill Mason's on time to-night.
             —*F. Bret Harte.*

UNCLE JOE.

I HAVE in memory a little story,
  That few indeed would care to tell but me;
'Tis not of love, nor fame, nor yet of glory,
  Although a little colored with the three;
In very truth, I think as much perchance,
At most tales disembodied from romance.

Joe lived about the village, and was neighbor
  To every one who had hard work to do;
If he possessed a genius, 'twas for labor.
  Most people thought ; but there were one or two,
Who sometimes said, when he arose to go,
"Come again and see us, again, Uncle Joe!

The "Uncle" was a courtesy they gave,
  And felt they could afford to give to him,
Just as the master makes of some good slave
  An Aunt Jemima, or an Uncle Jim ;
And of this dubious kindness Joe was glad :
Poor fellow, it was all he ever had!

A mile or so away he had a brother—
  A rich, proud man that people didn't hire ;
But Joe had neither sister, wife nor mother
  And baked his corn-cake at his cabin fire
After the day's work, hard for you or me,
But her was never tired—how could he be ?

The called him dull, but he had eyes of quickness
  For everybody that he could befriend ;
Said one and all, " How kind he is in sickness."
  But there, of course, his goodness had an end.
Another praise there was might have been given,
For one or more days out of every seven—

With his old pickaxe swung across his shoulder,
  And downcast eyes, and slow and sober tread,
He sought the place of graves, and each beholder
  Wondered, and asked some other who was dead ;
But when he digged all day, nobody thought
That he had done a whit more than he ought.

At length one winter, when the sunbeams slanted
  Faintly and cold across the churchyard snow,
The bell tolled out—alas! a grave was wanted,
  And all looked anxiously for Uncle Joe ;
His spade stood there against his own roof-tree
There was his pickaxe, too, but where was he ?

They called and called again, but no replying ;
  Smooth at the window, and about the door
The snow in cold and heavy drifts was lying.
  He didn't need the daylight any more.
One shook him roughly, and another said,
"As true as preaching, Uncle Joe is dead! "

And when they wrapped him in the linen, fairer,
  And finer too, than he had worn till then,
They found a picture—haply of the sharer,
  Of sunny hope some time ; or where or when
They did not care to know, but closed his eyes
And placed it in the coffin where he lies!

None wrote his epitaph, nor saw the beauty
  Of the pure love that reached into the grave,
Nor how in unobtrusive ways of duty.
  He kept, despite the dark ; but men less brave
Have left great names, while not a willow bends
Above his dust—poor Joe, he had no friends!

ALEC YEATON'S SON.

THE wind it wailed, the wind it moaned,
  And the white caps flecked the sea ;
"An' I would to God," the skipper groaned,
  "I had not my boy with me!"

Snug in the stern sheets, little John
  Laughed as the scud swept by;
But the skipper's sunburnt cheek grew wan
  As he watched the wicked sky.

"Would he were at his mother's side!"
  And the skipper's eyes were dim.
"Good Lord in heaven, if ill betide,
  What would become of him!

"For me—my muscles are as steel,
  For me let hap what may;
I might make shift upon this keel
  Until the break o' day.

"But he, he is so weak and small,
  So young, scarce learned to stand—
O pitying Father of us all,
  I trust him in Thy hand!

"For Thou, who markest from on high
  A sparrow's fall—each one!
Surely, O Lord, Thou'lt have an eye
  On Alec Yeaton's son!"

Then, helm hard aport, right straight he sailed
  Toward the headland light:
The wind it moaned, the wind it wailed,
  And black, black fell the night.

Then burst a storm to make one quail
  Though housed from winds and waves—
They who could tell about that gale
  Must rise from watery graves!

Sudden it came, as sudden went;
  Ere half the night was sped,
The winds were hushed, the waves were spent,
  And the stars shone overhead.

Now, as the morning mist grew thin,
  The folk on Gloucester shore
Saw a little figure floating in
  Secure, on a broken oar!

Up rose the cry, "A wreck! a wreck!
  Pull mates, and waste no breath—"
They knew it, though 'twas but a speck
  Upon the edge of death!

Long did they marvel in the town
  At God his strange decree,
That let the stalwart skipper drown,
  And the little child go free!"
        —*Thomas Bailey Aldrich.*

THE TRAMP.

LEMME sit down a minute, a stone's got in my
  shoe;
Don't you commence your cussin', I ain't done
  nothin' to you.
Yes, I'm a tramp. What of it? Folks say we
  ain't no good,
But tramps has to live, I reckon, though folks
  don't think we should.
Once I was strong and handsome, had plenty of
  cash and clothes;
That was afore I tippled and gin got into my
  nose.
Down in Lehigh Valley me and my people grew,
I was a blacksmith, cap'en—yes, and a good one,
  too;
Me and my wife and Nellie—Nellie was just sixteen,
She was the pootiest creature the valley had ever
  seen.
Beaux? Why, she had a dozen—had 'em from
  near and fur.
But they were mostly farmers, none of 'em suited
  her.

There was a city stranger, young, handsome and
  tall.
Damn him—I wish I had him strangled agin that
  wall
He was the man for Nellie—she didn't know no
  ill;
Mother she tried to stop it, but you know a young
  girl's will,
Well, it's the same old story—common enough
  you'll say,
He was a soft-tongued devil, and he got her to run
  away.
More than a month after we heard from the poor
  young thing;
He'd gone away and left her without a wedding
  ring.
Back to her home we brought her, back to her
  mother's side,
Fill'd with a raging fever—she fell at my feet and
  died.
Frantic with shame and trouble, her mother began to sink—
Dead—in less than a fortnight—that's when I took
  to drink.
Gimme one glass, Curnel, and then I'll be on my
  way.
I'll tramp till I find that scoundrel, if it takes till
  the Judgment Day.

THE OLD WIFE'S KISS.

THE funeral service ended the voice of prayer had
  ceased.
It was an aged pilgrim, whose soul had been released.
The neighbors were conversing in whispered un-
  dertone,
Yet the old wife at the coffin-head in silence stood
  alone.

Her wet eyes gazed intently upon the shriveled
  face.
The furrowed history written there her soul could
  plainly trace.
She saw in that sad moment his whole life pictured there,
Old-age, strong manhood, bouyant youth, when
  both were young and fair.

Again a bright hope sprang to life, a moment—
  but the pall
Recalled her desolation, her loneliness and all.
No home, no husband, children gone; oh, agony!
  oh, pain!
The fallen Keystone of that arch could ne'er be
  placed again.

And 'mid the shattered fragments she bowed her
  trembling head
And stretched her withered piteous hands in silence toward the dead,
And gazed in dumb expectancy—then left one lingering kiss,
Expressing every sentiment that fills a life like
  this;

A kiss of love, of sorrow, of memory, of farewell;
A kiss with life's whole history all crowded in its
  spell.
But look! whence comes that gayish hue, that
  sudden gasp for breath?
The limp hands fell, the form sinks down into the
  arms of death!

Oh, say not spirits meet and kiss. The worn-out
  thread of life
Snapped in the ecstacy of bliss when husband
  claimed his wife.
Oh, say not that his unseen hands were clasped in
  grateful prayer,
When that grand kiss released her soul and gave
  it to his care.
        —*Eliza Lamb Martyn.*

JOHN WHITE'S THANKSGIVING.

"THANKSGIVING !—for what ?"
   —and he muttered a curse—
"For the plainest of food
   and an empty purse;
For a life of hard work
   and the shabbiest clothes ?
But it's idle to talk
   of a poor man's woes !
Let the rich give thanks,
   it is they who can ;
There is nothing in life
   for a laboring man."
So said John White
   to his good wife Jane,
And o'er her face
   stole a look of pain.
"Nothing, dear John ?"
   and he thought again ;
Then glanced more kindly
   down on Jane.
"I was wrong," he said ;
   "I'd forgotten you.
And I've my health,
   and the baby, too."
And the baby crowed—
   'twas a bouncing boy—
And o'er Jane's face
   came a look of joy ;
And she kissed her John
   as he went away ;
And he said to himself,
   as he worked that day :
"I was wrong, very wrong ;
   I'll not grumble again,
I should surely be thankful
   for baby and Jane."

WHO'S DEAD.

EXCUSE me for stopping you here, sir ; I'd like
 just a word if you please ;
There's a crape on the front door yonder and a
 hearse standing under the trees.
Perhaps you're a friend of the dead, sir—I see
 you've a band on your hat—
And I'd like just to ask you a question, Who's
 dead in the Kennedy flat ?

Acquaint with the folks ? Well, yes, rather ;
 p'r'aps better than most as is there ;
There's Dick, and there's Sam and there's Billy,
 and mother—no wonder you stare.
It slipped out afore I could help it ; I ain't been
 myself all the day—
You may have heard tell of the bad 'un, the
 drunkard, as went away ?

You've not ? Well, it's like them three fellows to
 hide all they can of my shame,
And just like that dearest of mothers to let no one
 blacken my name !
It's soiled enough, God is my witness, but cleanse
 it I will if I can ;
I've done with the whiskey forever, and come
 back to mother—a man !

Come back ! Aye, to stand here and tremble and
 gaze at the crape on the door.
Mebbe him as is dead might be living had the
 truant but come back before.
P'r'aps the thoughts of a wrongdoin' brother
 made him grieve when the Doc wasn't there,
And they say that in sickness a heartache can
 undo the tenderest care.

Come, tell me, who's gone at the flat, sir ? Nay,
 don't think by shaking your head
That you're letting a fellow down easy, for I
 know that there's one of 'em dead.
They all was good boys to their mother and either
 is bound to be missed,
Though to tell you the truth I half fancy she'd cry
 more for me than the rest.

That is always the way with the women ; the one
 that's deserving no love
Gets into their hearts' warmest corner, their
 prayers to the Father above.
But when brother's coffin is fastened I'll lay her
 dear face on my own
And tell her that God's wrought a wonder, to
 make up for him that has flown.

And when this new grief's a bit over I'll tell—
 just to show her, you know,
That the liquor as hardened my life left my heart
 still as soft as the snow—
I will tell how, wherever I wandered, her voice
 seemed to ring in my ears ;
How I've slept with her lips on my forehead and
 waked with my eyes full of tears.

For we parted, you know, not in anger ; I just
 went away for a time,
Telling mother my bad reputation made staying
 at home seem a crime.
I had no ambition, nor nothing ; but soon a new
 life I began,
And now I am here in her sorrow—her very ideal
 of a man !

My words seem kind of affectin', I see that for her
 you can feel :
There's too many mothers' hearts breaking with
 grief that they try to conceal :
But come in the house, and I fancy you'll see
 through the flood of her tears
The smile that has lived in my mem'ry all through
 these unfortunate years.

Eh ? What ? God above ! You are ghastly ! Don't
 say—Oh I see't in your face !
Make way for the drunkard, good people—fit now
 for a mother's embrace.

 * * * * * * *

The same ! See the smile on her face, sir ; but
 God's kissed away every tear.
I don't care what joys are in heaven, her angel
 thoughts now are right here.
       —*Thomas Frost.*

THE BOY HERO.

CHILDREN, listen to the story I will try my best
 to tell,
Of a hero brave as any that in battle nobly fell.
It was not in long-past ages, nor in country far
 away,
But the scene was Bristol city, and it was the
 other day ;
And the hero of my story was a boy but six years
 old,
Yet I think his name is worthy to be written up
 in gold.

Johnnie Carr and Willie Stephens went out play-
 ing in the street ;
Willie was two years the younger, and his face
 was pale and sweet :
Little Willie ! pretty Willie ! many a stranger
 passing by
Turned and smiled at little Willie with his wide
 blue wondering eye.

Johnnie Carr was strong and rosy, curly haired
  and hazel-eyed,
Bright and merry—who can wonder Johnnie was
  his mother's pride ?
Yet there was a spark of mischief lurking in
  those dimpled cheeks,
Though you never could be angry at his little
  thoughtless freaks.

Willie's hoop, see, he has taken, running laughing on before;
Little Willie tries to catch him, till he scarce can
  follow more;
Then the tears come, yet he follows with his little
  weary feet,
Follows to the fields and hedges, far beyond the
  busy street;
Then he sits beside the pathway, crying in his
  childish woe,
Weeping sadly for his mother, asking home again
  to go.
Chilly is the autumn evening, quickly falls the
  deepening shade;
Johnnie takes the little hand and bids him not
  to be afraid.
So a little while they wander, but they miss the
  homeward track,
And the wind is blowing colder, and the night
  comes drear and black.
'Oh, I am so tired, Johnnie!' little Willie sadly
  cries;
'And I'm cold and hungry, Johnnie!' Tears are
  now in Johnnie's eyes;
He has teased the little fellow, but he's full of
  sad remorse.
'Get up, Willie,' he is saying; 'get up; I will be
  your horse.'
Then upon his back he took him, staggering on
  beneath his load.—
Staggering just a little distance on the dark and
  friendless road;
But the burden was too heavy, and he set poor
  Willie down ;—
Sorely puzzled now was Johnnie how to get to
  Bristol town.
'Don't be frightened, Willie,' said he ; 'we will
  stop out here to-night,
And we'll find our way directly when there
  comes the morning light.'
On a gate they sat a little ; then said Johnnie,
  'Let us look ;
Perhaps within the field behind us we may find
  a sheltered nook.'
So into the field they clambered, and a sheltered
  nook they found,
Where the little tired fellows laid them down
  upon the ground.
But the sodden earth was chilly, and they shiv-
  ered lying there,
Little Willie, cold and hungry, sobbing for his
  mother's care.

Then got up our little hero—he was only six years
  old,
Yet he could not bear that Willie should be crying
  with the cold.
In his brave love all unconscious, just in simple,
  childish guise,
Never thinking he is sharing in a mightier Sacrifice,
Johnnie took his little jacket, laid it down to make
  a bed,
And his other clothing simply over little Willie
  spread ;
Then himself laid down uncovered (save his little
  socks and shirt),
Thinking, 'I am strong, but Willie's very small,
  and shan't be hurt.'
With a start there came to Johnnie sudden
  thought of One who cares
For His children, and he whispered, 'Willie, we
  forgot our prayers.'

There they knelt, the little fellows side by side
  upon the sod,
With their simply-lisped 'Our Father' casting all
  their care on God.
Then once more they lay enfolded in each other's
  arms so fast,
And the night wind bleak and cruel froze them
  with its chilling blast.

See those fathers, half distracted, friends and
  neighbors pressing near,
Into every nook and corner how, with eager haste
  they peer !
See those mothers, broken-hearted for their darlings, how they gaze
Wheresoe'er the friendly lanterns high uplifted
  cast their rays !
Aye, but chiefly, as the tide falls, longing much
  yet dreading more,
Hollow-eyed, the oozy mud-banks of the river
  they explore.
(How by hour of chill and darkness (oh, how slow
  the morning light !)
In their hopeless search they wander all that long
  and dreadful night.

Is it morning; they have found them. Lo! a la-
  borer on his way
Came upon them, as still folded in each other's
  arms, they lay.
They are breathing, barely breathing, all unconscious, cold as stone ;
Noble Johnnie! pretty Willie! yes, the life has
  not quite flown.
And they take them to a cottage, and they chafe
  each frozen limb;
Little Willie has been covered ; there is better
  hope for him,
And the mothers stand there watching, and their
  tears are falling fast.
Little Willie's eyelids tremble ; yes, there's hope
  for him at last !
See, the warm milk he has swallowed ! See, he
  sighs a little sigh!
Then he smiles, as on his mother he uplifts his
  large blue eye.
But the little hero, Johnnie—ah ! they chafe his
  limbs in vain !
Never shall his merry laughter echo through the
  house again.
Faint and fainter comes his breathing, marble-
  white that open brow,
Who will dare to speak of comfort to those strick-
  en watchers now ?
'O my Johnnie! O my Johnnie! speak to me one
  little word!'
Sobbed the mother; but I know not whether
  Johnnie ever heard.
Yet at once, as one awaking, with his eyelids
  open wide,
Just one word he whispered faintly—it was 'Wil-
  lie!'—then he died.

In the churchyard Johnnie's sleeping, underneath
  the grassy mould;
No one puts a stone upon it, lettered with the tale
  in gold—
''Neath this stone a little hero, Johnnie Carr of
  Bristol, lies,
Who, to save his little playmate, gave his life a
  sacrifice.'

Children, think how, when the nations gather
  round the mighty throne,
He Who gave His life for others will claim Johnnie for His own.
Think how full of strange sweet wonder will the
  gracious tidings be—
'What thou didst to little Willie, that I count as
  done to me.'

          —*Right Rev. William Walsham How.*

SELLING THE BABY.

BENEATH a shady elm tree
Two little brown-haired boys
Were complaining to each other
That they couldn't make a noise.
" And it's all that horrid baby,"
Cried Johnny, looking glum,
" She makes an awful bother;
I 'most wish she hadn't come.

" If a boy runs through the kitchen,
Still as a mouse can creep,
Norah says, ' Now do be aisy,
For the baby's gone to sleep! '
And when, just now, I asked mamma
To fix my new straw cap,
She said she really couldn't
Till the baby took her nap! "

" I've been thinking we might sell her—"
Fred thrust back his curly hair;
" Mamma calls her ' Little Trouble ! '
So I don't believe she'd care.
We will take her down to Johnson's;
He keeps candy at his store,
And I wouldn't wonder, truly,
If she'd bring a pound or more;

" For he asked me if I'd sell her
When she first came, but, you see,
Then I didn't know she'd bother,
So I told him, 'No, sir-ree! '
He may have her now, and welcome;
I don't want her any more.
Get the carriage round here, Johnny,
And I'll fetch her to the door."

To the cool green-curtained bedroom
Freddy stole with noiseless feet,
Where mamma had left her baby
Fast asleep, serene and sweet.
Soft he bore her to the carriage,
All unknowing, little bird!
While of these two young kidnappers
Not a sound had mamma heard.

Down the street the carriage trundled;
Soundly still the baby slept;
Over two sun-browned boy-faces
Little sober shadows crept;
They began to love the wee one.
" Say," said Johnny, " don't you think
He will give for such a baby
Twenty pounds as quick as wink ?"

" I'd say fifty," Fred responded,
With his brown eyes downward cast.
" Here's the store; it doesn't seem's though
We had come so awful fast!"
Through the door they pushed the carriage;
" Mister Johnson, we thought maybe
You would—wouldn't—would you—would you—
Would you like to buy a baby ?"

Merchant Johnson's eye were twinkling;
" Well, I would; just set your price,
Will you take your pay in candy?
I have some that's very nice.
But before we bind the bargain,
I would like to see the child! "
Johnny lifted up the afghan;
Baby woke and cooed and smiled.

" It's a trade!" cried Merchant Johnson;
" How much candy for the prize ?"
Fred and Johnny looked at baby,
Then into each other's eyes.
All forgotten was the bother
In the light of baby's smile,
And they wondered if mamma had
Missed her daughter all the while.

" Candy's sweet, but baby's sweeter,"
Spoke up sturdy little Fred.
" 'Cause she is our own and onliest
Darling sister," Johnny said,
" So I guess we'd better keep her,
But if we should ask him—maybe
When he knows you'd like to have one,
God will send you down a baby ! "

Merchant Johnson laughed, and kindly
Ran their small hands o'er with sweet
Ere they wheel the baby homeward,
Back along the quiet street;
And mamma (who had not missed them)
Smiled to hear the little tale,
How they went to sell the baby,
How they didn't make the sale.
—Ada Carleton.

THE LIGHT ON DEADMAN'S BAR.

THE light-house keeper's daughter looked out
across the bay
To the north, where, hidden in tempest, she
knew the mainland lay;
The waters were lashed to fury by the wind that
swept the sea.
"Father won't think of crossing in a storm like
this," said she;
"'Twould be death to undertake it—and yet, when
he thinks of the light
He may try to reach the island. Perhaps," and
her eyes grew bright
With the thought, " if I go and light it before the
night shuts down,
He may see it from the mainland, and stay all
night in the town.
I'm sure that I can do it," she whispered under
her breath,
And her heart was strong with the courage that
comes at the thought of death
When it threatens to strike our loved ones.
" For father's sake," cried she,
I'll light the lamp and tend it. Perhaps some
ship at sea
May see it shine through the darkness and steer
by its warning star
Past the rocks and reef of danger that lie on
Deadman's Bar."

She climbed the winding stairway with never a
thought of fear,
Though the demon of the tempest seemed shouting in her ear;
She seemed to feel the tower in the wild wind
reel and rock,
And it shivered from foot to turret in the great
waves' thunder shock;
But she thought not so much of danger to herself
as to those at sea,
And the father off on the mainland, as up the
stair climbed she,
Till at last she stood in the turret before the
lamp whose light
Must be kindled to flash its warning across the
stormy night.

'Twas an easy task to light it, and soon its ray
shone out
Through the murky gloom that gathered the closing day about;
But a fear rose up in her bosom as the light began to burn—
Could she set the wheels in motion that made the
great lamp turn ?
If the light in the tower turned not, those who
saw it out at sea
Might think it was the North Point beacon or the
light on St Marie,

And woe to the ships whose courses were steered
  by a *steady* light
From the point where a *turning* signal should
  show its star at night

"If only my father had told me how to start the
  wheels!" she cried,
As she sought to put them in motion; but all in
  vain she tried
To set the great lamp turning; the stubborn
  wheels stood still.
"It *shall* turn!" she cried; "it *must* turn!" and
  strong of heart and will,
She roused to the task before her, and with her
  hands she swung
The great lamp in a circle on the arm from which
  it hung.

Now it was flashing seaward, and now it flashed
  toward the land,
And those who saw the beacon would think not
  that the hand
Of a little girl was turning the light up there in
  the storm,
To warn the ships from the dangers with which
  the low reefs swarm.
Steadily round she swung it as darkness fell over
  the sea,
"Father will see it, believing the wheels are at
  work," laughed she.

Darkness closed in about her as round and round
  she swung
The lamp in its iron socket The tempest-demons
  sung
Their fierce, wild songs above her; below the maddened waves
Howled at the light that was cheating the pitiless
  sea of graves.
No thought of fear came to her up there alone in
  the night—
Her thoughts were all of the sailors and the turning of the light.

The lonesome hours went by her on weary feet
  and slow;
Sometimes, before she knew it, her drowsy lids
  drooped low;
Then she thought of what might happen if she let
  the light stand still
Was like a voice that roused her and sent a
  mighty thrill
Tingling through all her being. So, steadily
  round she swung
The lamp, and smiled to see its gleam across the
  dark night flung.

"I wonder if father sees it. If he does, he's glad,"
  thought she;
"It may be that brother Benny is somewhere out
  at sea.
Who knows but what I am doing may save his
  ship and him?"
And then, for one little moment, the brave girl's
  eyes grew dim,
But her heart and arm grew stronger with purpose high and grand
As she thought of the sailor brother whose fate
  she might hold in her hand.

So, with hands that never faltered through all
  that long, long night
She kept the great lamp turning till broke the
  ruddy light
Of morning over the waters. "Now I can sleep,"
  said she,
With one last thought of her father and the
  brother out at sea.
Then the hands that were, oh, so weary! fell
  heavily at her side,
And she slept to dream of the beacon of the turning of the tide.

When she woke from her long, deep slumber the
  sun was high in the sky;
Her father sat by her bedside, and another was
  standing by:
"Benny," she cried, in gladness," did you see the
  light last night?
I thought of you while I turned it, and oh, I hoped
  you might!"

"My brave little sister," he answered, "do you
  know what you did last night?
You saved the lives of two score men when you
  tended Deadman's Light.
'Twas a grand night's work, my sister, a brave
  night's work to save
Two score of home-bound fishermen from a yawn-
  ing ocean grave.
Over there on the mainland they're talking of you
  to-day
As the girl that saved the good ship Jane, 'God
  bless the child!' they say;
And in many a home they'll speak, dear, your
  name in prayer to-night,
As they think of what they owe to her who tended
  Deadman's Light."

                             Eben E. Rexford.

THE STORY OF FAITH.

A RUSTLE of robes as the anthem
  Soared gently away on the air—
The Sabbath morn's service was over,
  And briskly I stepped down the stair;
When, close in a half-illumin'd corner,
  Where the tall pulpit's stairway came down,
Asleep crouched a tender wee maiden
  With hair like a shadowy crown.

Quite puzzled was I by the vision,
  But gently to wake her I spoke,
When, at the first word, the sweet damsel
  With one little gasp straight awoke.
"What brought you here, fair little angel?
  She answered with voice like a bell.
"I turn tus I've got a sick mamma,
  And I went on to please pray her well!"

"Who told you?" began I; she stopped me.
  "Don't nobody told me at all;
And papa can't see, tos he's cryin';
  And 'sides, sir, I isn't so small;
I's been here before with mamma—
  We tummed when you ringed the big bell;
And ev'ry time I'se heard oo prayin'
  For lots o' sick folks to dit well."

Together we knelt on the stairway
  As humbly I asked the Great Power
To give back her health to the mother,
  And banish breavement's dark hour,
I finished the simple petition,
  And paused for a moment—and then
A sweet little voice at my elbow,
  Lisped softly a gentle "Amen!"

Hand in hand we turned our steps homeward;
  The little maid's tongue knew no rest;
She prattled and mimmicked and caroled—
  The shadow was gone from her breast.
And lo! when we reached the fair dwelling,
  The nest of my golden-haired waif,
We found that the dearly loved mother
  Was past the dreaded crisis,—was safe.

They listened, amazed at my story,
  And wept o'er their darling's strange quest,
While the arms of the pale, loving mother
  Drew the brave little head to her breast
With eyes that were brimming and grateful
  They thanked me again and again;
Yet I know in my heart that the blessing
  Was won by that gentle "Amen!"

THE PREACHER'S VACATION.

The old man went to meetin', for the day was
bright and fair,
Tho' his limbs were very totterin' and 'twas
hard to travel there;
But he hungered for the gospel, so he trudged the
weary way,
On the road so rough and dusty, 'neath the summer's burning ray.

By and by he reached the building, to his soul a
holy place,
Then he paused and wiped the sweat-drops off his
thin and wrinkled face;
But he looked around bewildered, for the old bell
did not toll.
All the doors were shut and bolted, and he did not
see a soul.

So he leaned upon his crutches, and he said
"What does it mean?"
And he looked this way and that, till it seemed
almost a dream;
He had walked the dusty highway, and he
breathed a heavy sigh,
Just to go once more to meetin' ere the summons
came to die.

But he saw a little notice tacked upon the meetin'
door,
So he limped along to read it, and he read it o'er
and o'er,
Then he wiped his dusty glasses, and he read it
o'er again,
Till his limbs began to tremble and his eyes began to pain.

As the old man read the notice, how it made his
spirit burn,
"Pastor absent on vacation; church is closed till
his return."
Then he staggered slowly backward, and he sat
him down to think.
For his soul was stirred within him, till he thought
his heart would sink.

So he mused aloud and wondered, to himself so-
liloquized:
"I have lived to almost eighty, and was never so
surprised.
As I read that oddest notice stickin' on the
meetin'-door,
I astir off on a vacation'; never heard the like
before.

Why, when I first joined the meetin', very many
years ago,
Preachers traveled on the circuit, in the heat and
through the snow,
If they got their clothes and victuals, 'twas but
little cash they got,
They said nothing bout vacation, but were happy
with their lot.

"Would the farmer leave his cattle, or the shep-
herd leave his sheep?
Who would give them care and shelter or provide
them food to eat?
So it strikes me very sing'lar when a man of holy
hands
Thinks he needs to have vacation, and forsakes
his tender lambs.

"Tell me, when I tread the valley and go up the
shining height,
Will I hear no angels singing—will I see no gleaming light?
Will the golden harps be silent—will I meet no
welcome there?
Why, the thought is most distractin'; 'twould be
more than I could bear.

"Tell me, when I reach the city over on the other
shore,
Will I find a little notice tacked upon the golden
door,
Tellin' me, 'mid dreadful silence, writ in words
that cut and burn,
Jesus absent on vacation, Heaven closed till His
return?'"

WHISPERIN' BILL.

So you're takin' the census, mister? There's
three of us livin' still,
My wife, and I, an' our only son, that folks call
Whisperin' Bill;
But Bill couldn't tell ye his name, sir, an' so it's
hardly worth givin',
For ye see a bullet killed his mind an' left his body
livin'.

Set down fer a minute, mister. Ye see Bill was
only fifteen
At the time of the war, an' as likely a boy as ever
this world has seen;
An' what with the news o' battles lost, the
speeches an' all the noise,
I guess every farm in the neighborhood lost a part
of its crop o' boys.

'Twas harvest time when Bill left home; every
stalk in the fields of rye
Seemed to stand tiptoe to see him off an' wave him
a fond good-bye;
His sweetheart was here with some other girls,—
the sassy little miss!
An' pretendin' she wanted to whisper 'n his ear,
she gave him a rousin' kiss.

Oh, he was a han'some feller, an' tender an' brave
an' smart,
An' tho' he was bigger than I was, the boy had a
woman's heart.
I couldn't control my feelin's, but I tried with all
my might,
An' his mother an' me stood a-cryin' till Bill was
out o' sight.

His mother she often told him when she knew he
was goin' away
That God would take care o' him, maybe, if he
didn't fergit to pray;
An' on the bloodiest battlefields, when bullet-
whizzed in the air,
An' Bill was a-fightin' desperate, he used to
whisper a prayer.

Oh, his comrades has often told me that Bill never
flinched a bit
When every second a gap in the ranks told where
a ball had hit.
An' one night when the field was covered with the
awful harvest of war,
They found my boy 'mongst the martyrs o' the
cause he was fightin' for.

His fingers were clutched in the dewy grass—oh,
no, sir, he wasn't dead,
But he lay sort o' helpless an' crazy with a rifle
ball in his head.
An' if Bill had really died that night, I'd give all
I've got worth givin';
For ye see the bullet had killed his mind an' left
his body livin'.

An officer wrote and told us how the boy had been
hurt in the fight,
But he said that the doctors reckoned they could
bring him around all right.
An' then we heard from a neighbor, disabled at
Malvern Hill,
That he thought in a course of a week or so he'd
be comin' home with Bill.

We was that anxious t' see him we'd set up an'
talk o' nights
Till the break o' day had dimmed the stars an' put
out the northern lights;
We waited and watched for a month or more, an'
the summer was nearly past,
When a letter came one day that said they'd
started fer home at last.

I'll never fergit the day Bill came,—'twas harvest
time again;
An' the air blown over the yellow fields was sweet
with the scent o' the grain;
The dooryard was full o' the neighbors, who had
come to share our joy,
An' all of us sent up a mighty cheer at the sight o'
that soldier boy.

An' all of a sudden somebody said: "My God!
don't the boy know his mother?"
An' Bill stood a-whisperin', fearful like, an' starin'
from one to another;
"Don't be afraid, Bill," said he to himself, as he
stood in his coat o' blue,
"Why, God'll take care o' you, Bill, God'll take
care o' you."

He seemed to be loadin' an' firin' a gun, an' to act
like a man who hears
The awful roar o' the battlefield a-soundin' in his
ears;
I saw that the bullet had touched his brain an'
somehow made it blind,
With the picture o' war before his eyes an' the
fear o' death in his mind.

I grasped his hand, an' says I to Bill, "Don't ye
remember me?
I'm yer father—don't ye know me? How frightened ye seem to be!"
But the boy kep' a-whisperin' to himself, as if
'twas all he knew
"God'll take care o' you, Bill, God'll take care o'
you."

He's never known us since that day, nor his
sweetheart, an' never will;
Father an' mother an' sweetheart are all the same
to Bill.
An' many's the time his mother sets up the whole
night through,
An' smooths his head, and says: "Yes, Bill,
God'll take care o' you."

Unfortunit? Yes, but we can't complain. It's a
livin' death more sad
When the body clings to a life o' shame an' the
soul has gone to the bad;
An' Bill is out o' the reach o' harm an' danger of
every kind;
We only take care of his body, but God takes care
o' his mind.
                                    —*Irving Bacheller.*

A BRAVE WOMAN.

I TALKED with a stalwart young seaman last
week on Ratcliffe Highway;
He belonged to the crew of a steamer that was
wrecked in Aberdour Bay,
And I asked him if he would mind telling the way
he was saved from the sea?
Then (excepting the rhyme) he narrated the following story to me:

"Well, you see, we had started for home, sir, and
were anxious to get on our way,
When it came on to blow big guns, sir, as we stood
off Aberdour Bay;
But our craft was so sturdy a steamer, that we
laughed and thought light of the gale,
For no matter how angry the weather, we never
had known her to fail.

"But accidents weaken the strongest, and our
skipper's brow and face grew long,
When a message came up from below, sir, that
the engines had all gone wrong.
Then we set to and hoisted what canvas we
thought that the vessel would bear,
And tried to beat clear of the bay, sir, for the gale
was driving in there.

"But, no; it was useless our trying, for the wind
blew so frightfully hard
That on to the shore, to leeward, the ship drifted
yard after yard;
The skipper roared, 'Let go the anchor!' We did
so, our drifting was checked;
But we knew if the cable should snap, sir, the ship
would be certainly wrecked.

"The billows dashed over, around us, as though
mad that we held our own;
Then 'crack?' 'twas the cable parting, and our
hearts seemed turned into stone;
Once more we were driven shorewards, this time
at a furious rate;
There was nothing could possibly check us, so the
steamer rushed on to her fate.

"Then we felt her quiver and shudder, as she
struck on the pebbly beach,
And we looked with despair at the shore, sir, that,
living, we could not reach;
For the surf was boiling and hissing, and dashing
with all its force,
And no man could have swum to the land, sir, not
if he'd the strength of a horse.

"There was only one woman ashore there, and
we'd hardly a glimmer of hope,
Yet I managed to screw up my spirits, and determined to throw her a rope;
I tried, but too great was the distance; and, despairing, I saw it fall short;
But that woman dashed into the surf, sir, and the
next time I threw it 'twas caught.

"God bless her! she caught up that rope, sir, and
in spite of the boisterous sea,
She wound it three times round her body, and up
from the water went she;
And she beckoned us each to come quickly, but
we thought that 'twould be but in vain;
'For no woman alive,' we murmured, 'can stand
such a terrible strain!'

"But yet we would try, for 'twas certain delay
meant a terrible death;
So we started a man on the voyage, whilst the
rest of the crew held their breath;

There, 'hand over hand' he traveled, whilst as
    firm as a rock stood she,
Till at length the seaman was saved, sir, from the
    clutch of the merciless sea.

"Then one after the other we followed, till the
    whole of the crew were on land;
Oh! you ought to have seen us struggling for a
    grasp of that brave woman's hand!
It may seem very foolish to you, sir, but I felt
    almost ready to cry;
And there wasn't a sailor amongst us but what
    had a tear in his eye.

"Every true-hearted man or woman will praise
    this true heroine's act;
It isn't a jumble of fiction, but a plain, undeniable
    fact;
I declare she's as plucky a woman as any of
    which I have read;
Quite fit to take rank with Grace Darling and the
    Women of Mumbles Head "
                                —John F. Nicholls.

"FLAG THE TRAIN."

The last words of Engineer Edward Kennar,
who died in a railroad accident near St. Johns-
ville, N. Y., April 18, 1887.

Go, flag the train, boys, flag the train!
    Nor waste the time on me;
But leave me by my shattered cab;
    'Tis better thus to be!
It was an awful leap, boys,
    But the worst of it is o'er;
I hear the Great Conductor's call
    Sound from the farther shore.

I hear sweet notes of angels, boys,
    That seem to say: "Well done!"
I see a golden city there,
    Bathed in a deathless sun;
There is no night, nor sorrow, boys,
    No wounds nor bruises there;
The way is clear—the engineer
    Rests from his life's long care.

Ah! 'twas a fearful plunge, my lads;
    I saw, as in a dream,
Those dear, dear faces looming up
    In yonder snowy stream;
Down in the Mohawk's peaceful depths
    Their image rose and smiled,
E'en as we took the fatal leap,
    Oh God—my wife! my child!

Well, never mind! I ne'er shall see
    That wife and child again;
But hasten, hasten, leave me, boys!
    For God's sake, flag the train!
Farewell, bright Mohawk! and farewell
    My cab, my comrades all;
I'm done for, boys, but hasten on,
    And sound the warning call!

Oh what a strange, strange tremor this
    That steals unceasing on!
Will those dear ones I've cherished so
    Be cared for when I'm gone?
Farewell, ye best beloved, farewell!
    I've died not all in vain—
Thank God! The other lives are saved;
Thank God! They've flagged the train!
                            — William B. Chisholm.

KIT CARSON'S WIFE.

One winter eve, when cabin's bright
With the crimson flash of the log-fire's light,
And the soft snow sleeps on the prairie's breast,
They gather—the frontier scouts of the West—
And, speaking sometimes with bated breath
Of wars of the border, and deeds of death,
They crown their stories of reckless strife
With the famous ride of Kit Carson's wife.

For into a Sioux village one day,
From Dixon, a hundred miles away,
A horseman reached the chieftain's tent,
Dismounted, staggered and gasped: "I'm sent
With sorrowful news from the pale-face town.
Kit Carson the scout is stricken down,
And before he bids farewell to life
He would see the face of his Indian wife."

She heard that story—the chieftain's child—
Her bronze face whitened, her glance grew wild;
She grasped her deer-skin cloak and felt
The pistols were safe in her wampum belt;
She uttered only a smothered moan,
And the scout and the chieftain stood alone.

Her pony snorted; she grasped his mane,
And the fleetest mustang that pressed the plain,
Turning away from the sunset light,
Sped like an arrow into the night,
And the flanks threw backward a glistening foam
As she headed her horse to her husband's home.

Oh, sing not to me of Lochinvar,
Or of reckless rides in glorious war!
But, oh! if ever perchance you hear
Of Sheridan, Graves, or Paul Revere—
Of all that galloped to deathless life,
Just speak the name of Kit Carson's wife.

The stars leaped out in the boundless sky,
And the girl looked up as the moon flashed by—
The terrified moon, in a terrible race,
Keeping time to her pony's pace!
She heard the hoot of the lonely owl,
Louder and louder, piercing the air,
Till her throbbing heart moaned a pitiful prayer,
For, grasping her pistol and looking back,
The Indian girl saw wolves on her track.

The foremost fell with a shot in his heart,
And his comrades tore him part from part
While the horse flashed faster over the plain
With the girl's dark face in his tangled mane,
Over the trackless prairies, away,
Galloping into the new-born day.
The first faint rays of the daybreak dim
Showed her upon the horizon's rim
An armed band of her people's foes,
Riding as fast as the north wind blows,
With the flash of the sun on the leader's plume—
A signal that sealed the maiden's doom.

But the daring blood of a noble race,
Like flames in a gloomy forest place,
Flushed redly into her Indian face,
And she caught the tomahawk at her side,
A toy in the blood of berries dyed—
Swung it aloft, and with panting breath
Galloped full in the front of death.

Over each mustang every foe
Swerved like lightning, bending low;
Thro' the band, that parted to right and left,
A clear wide path the maiden cleft,
And an instant more she had passed them by
And was riding alone into the eastern sky.

The terrified braves looked back on her there,
While the sunlight's glory over her hair
Shone like a halo, wonderful, grand!
Had she fled from the far-off spirit-land ?
Had she brought them blessings, or a blight ?
They shuddered and broke into sudden flight.

Into the streets of a cabin town—
Into the village riding down,
With fevered brain, and with glazing eyes,
And breath that fluttered with gasping sighs,
Still she urged on the faltering steed
That had served her well in her hour of need.
And the pony leaped as it felt the rein,
Galloped, staggered, and reeled again,
And just as it reached Kit Carson's door,
With work well done and with anguish o'er,
Fell to the earth and stirred no more.
An hour later the great scout died,
His faithful Indian wife at his side.
She only lingered a little while,
And followed him then with a happy smile.
Together they sleep in the self-same grave,
Where wildly the winds of winter rave,
And in summer the prairie flowers wave!

THE PAUPER'S CHRISTMAS EVE.

FOUR little heads were bent, one night, in consultation deep ;
Their mamma thought them safe abed—'twas time
they were fast asleep;
And one belonged to Mabel, with the hair and eyes
so black,
And one to blue-eyed Genevieve, and two to Ralph
Jack.

Four loving hearts beat high within the half-enlivened gloom
Around the fire in Genevieve's and Mabel's cozy
room;
The whispered talk ran on and on, as if it ne'er
would cease,
A council there of war they held—or rather, 'twas
of peace.

Because the time had nearly come for Christmas
bells to ring,
When cherished friends to cherished friends their
offerings would bring;
And so the time had fully come, for they four to
agree
About the best and nicest place to hold their
Christmas tree.

Said Jack: "Let's go and have it once upon the
great barn floor ;
And we will rear so high a one as ne'er was seen
before,
We'll trim and deck the whole place like a forest
grand and old,
And all dress up so thickly, that we need not mind
the cold."

Then whispered blue-eyed Genevieve: "The prettiest place for me
Is in the parlor warm and bright to have a Christmas tree ;
With holly wreaths and pretty flowers all smiling
gayly there,
And just a few good dainty friends our festival to
share."

Said black-eyed Mabel: "Well, I think the nicest
place for me
Is in the great big splendid church, where all can
hear and see ;
Where all can view the lovely gifts their friends
may give and get;
'Mid dresses gay and music sweet mine is the
grandest yet."

But so far not a single word the pale-browed Ralph
had said,
But soberly and silent sat, with thoughtful, low-
bowed head;
Till all at once each turned to him, a bright, inquiring face,
And one said, "Ralph, where do *you* think would
be the nicest place ?"

Then soft-eyed Ralph replied: "I know the places
you would set
Would all be very fine ; but I have found a better
yet,—
The oddest, strangest place, indeed, you'd ever
want to see,
And one where I have never heard of any Christmas tree.

"As we were driving yesterday—our mother sweet
and I—
We came unto the poor-house farm—and slowly
we went by ;
Some faces from the window looked, but none
were happy-bright;
One was so sad and lonely, that I dreamed of it all
night.

"O, Christmas must be dreary to the poor and
friendless one,
To think of others getting gifts, and ho to look for
none ;
The poor-house parlor, I should think (if such a
place there be),
Would make a good and proper place to hold our
Christmas tree.

"The presents we're expecting, we for once could
do without;
The price would buy each pauper there a pretty
gift, no doubt;
Our parents, they will help us, if we only ask them
right;
Now dream of this, and think of this, when we
have said Good-night."

Cold-bitter was the Christmas eve ; the wind was
loud and chill;
It chased the snow-flakes thin and white across
the plain and hill;
It stormed the poor-house windows, and it tramped
its noisy round,
Until the paupers shuddered as they heard the
dreary sound.

And many a poor one mused and grieved, with
saddened eyes and dim,
Of long-lost times when Christmas eve meant
something bright to him,
And when he had a warm, sweet home, and loved
ones waiting there.
With bright smiles kindled up with love, and gifts
by love made fair.

And tears were shed by eyes that were but too
well used to weep,
And memories much too pleasant then were
hushed in painful sleep;
And visions came of happy homes, where all was
warm and bright,
With Christmas trees well blossomed o'er, to cheer
the stormy night.

When up before the poor-house door, with bells
and laughter gay,
There drove in blithe and merry haste a heavily
laden sleigh;
Into the dingy parlor then swift rushed the merry
four,
And reared a tree and hung each branch with
splendid presents o'er.

Into the room the paupers came, with wonder
   well-nigh dumb,
And wondered what was coming now, or rather
   what had come;
And black-eyed Mabel read their names, in accents clear and gay,
And sturdy Jack and Genevieve the presents gave
   away.

And Ralph sat by, close watching, with his pale
   and thoughtful face,
Each present that was given, and each glad smile's
   sudden trace;
For every one was suited there and every eye was
   glad,
Each one forgetting, for a time, whatever grief he
   had.

Old Gran'ther Smith looked gorgeous in a tippet
   new and warm,
Aunt Huldah drew a new thick shawl about her
   wasted form;
And not a man or woman there, and not a girl or
   boy,
But had some pretty present, full of comfort or of
   joy.

And pale Misfortune never yet had worn so bright
   a face,
Since first the dreary poor-house walls had found
   that dreary place;
"I almost wish this evening," said the smiling
   overseer,
"That I was just a boarder, like, and not the
   landlord here."

Now years have gone; and Genevieve and Mabel,
   women grown,
Each in a happy home resides, with children of
   her own;
Jack is a brave sea-captain now, a-sailing to and
   fro,
And pale-browed Ralph is lying deep beneath the
   winter snow.

But many a seed of joy they sowed upon that
   winter night,
Has never ceased to grow and thrive with blossoms sweet and bright;
And all the grand and glorious good that their
   kind deeds have done,
Shall flash in living splendor when our earth and
   heaven are one.

AN OLD MAN'S STORY.

'Tis only an old man's story,—a tale we have oft
   heard told,
In a thousand forms and fancies, by the young as
   well as old,
A tale of a life dragged hellward, bound down by
   a demon's chain,
Till the friendly hand of temp'rance had rescued
   it back again!
Though only a child at the time, friends, I well remember the night
Of our first great temp'rance meeting—it came as
   an angel of light,
Midst the darkness of vile intemp'rance, its myr-
   iad crimes and sin;
A guiding light to the path of right, that all might
   enter in!
A hymn, a prayer, an address; then the chair-
   man's voice was heard
To call on any one present just to say but a warning word,

Our pastor rose, midst cheering, but he strongly
   denounced the new cause
As "a movement which none but fanatics (hear,
   hear, and loud applause)
Would engage in, to injure the business of such
   respectable men,
And break up the time-honored usage of the
   country—" but just then
I saw, whilst a death-like silence reigned, an old
   man slowly rise
On the platform and fix on the speaker the glance
   of his piercing eyes!
That look held the audience spell-bound, and I
   noticed my father's cheek
Turn deadly pale as the stranger paused before
   he began to speak.
At last, with an effort, the old man said, in accents
   low but clear:
"You've heard, friends, that I'm a fanatic, that I
   have no business here;
As men and Christians listen to truth, hear me
   and be just;
My life-sands fast are running out, and speak to-
   night I must!
O'er a beaconless sea I've journeyed, life's dearest hopes I've wrecked—
God knows how my heart is aching, as I now o'er
   the past reflect.
I'm alone, without friends or kindred, but it was
   not always so,
For I see away o'er that ocean wild, dear forms
   pass to and fro.
I once knew a doting mother's love, but I crushed
   her fond old heart,
(He seemed to look at some vision, with his quivering lips apart)
I once loved an angel creature with her laughing
   eyes so blue,
And the sweetest child that ever smiled, and a
   boy so brave and true!
Perhaps, friends, you will be startled, but these
   hands have dealt the blow
That severed the ties of kindred love, and laid
   those dear ones low.
Ah! yes, *I was once a fanatic*; yea. more— a
   fiend, for then
I sacrificed my home, my all, for the riots of a
   drink fiend's den.
One New Year's night I entered the hut, that
   charity gave, and found
My starving wife all helpless and shivering on the
   ground;
With a maddened cry I demanded food, then
   struck her a terrible blow;
'Food, food,' I yelled, 'quick, give me food, or by
   heaven out you go!'
Just then our babe from its cradle set up a famished wail,
My wife caught up the little form, with its face so
   thin and pale,
Saying, 'James! my once kind husband, you know
   we've had no food
For near a week. Oh, do not harm my Willie that's
   so good.'
With a wild Ha! ha! I seized them, and lifted the
   latch of the door;
The storm burst in, but I hurled them out in the
   tempest's wildest roar,
A terrible impulse bore me on, so I turned to my
   little lad,
And snatched him from his slumbering rest—the
   thought near drives me mad.
To the door I fiercely dragged him, grasping his
   slender throat,
And thrust him out, but his hand had caught the
   pocket of my coat,
I could not wrench his frenzied hold, so I hit him
   with my fist,
Then shutting the door upon his arm *it severed at
   the wrist.*

I awoke in the morn from a stupor and idly
  opened the door;
With a moan I started backward—two forms fell
  flat to the floor.
The blood like burning arrows shot right up to my
  dazed brain,
As I called my wife by the dearest words; but,
  alas! I called in vain.
The thought of my boy flashed on me, I imprinted
  one fervent kiss
On those frozen lips : then searched around, but
  from that black day to this
My injured boy I've never seen—" He paused
  awhile and wept,
And I saw the tears on my father's cheek as I
  closer to him crept.
Once more the old man faltering said, " Ten long,
  long years I served,
With an aching heart, in a felon's cell, the sentence I deserved ;
But there's yet a gleam of sunshine in my life's
  beclouded sky,
And I long to meet my loved ones in the better
  land on high!"
The pledge book lay on the table, just where the
  old man stood,
He asked the men to sign it, and several said they
  would.
"Aye, sign it—angels would sign it," he ex-
  claimed with a look of joy ;
" I'd sign it a thousand times in blood, if it would
  bring back my boy!"
My father wrote his name down whilst he trembled in every limb;
The old man scanned it o'er and o'er, then
  strangely glanced at him.
My father raised his left arm up—a cry, a convul-
  sive start—
Then an old man and his injured boy were sobbing heart to heart!
Ere the meeting closed that evening, each offered
  a fervent prayer,
And many that night, who saw the sight, rejoiced
  that they were there!

—*Milton Thompson.*

LOST.

SOME eight and twenty years ago, I knew
A little boy whose hair of golden hue,
In ringlets clustered round his childish face,
Like fairies dancing at their trysting place.
And oft his dark-blue eyes with gleeful gaze
In trusting childhood's happy glowing blaze
Looked up in mother's smiling face so fair,
As she in silence breathed the evening prayer
In beauty, dazzling, innocent, and bright,
His soul was mirrored in those gems of light.
O happy mother! couldest thou explore
Thy idol's future life, a burden more
Than tender love, or patient soul could bear,
Would crush thy heart; o'erwhelm thee in despair.

I oft have looked upon a stately oak,
Whose strength for years resisted nature's stroke,
While silently a poisonous canker worm
Sipped the foundation of the giant form,
And slow but sure the death seal I could see,
Was set upon the mighty forest tree.
And oft I've rambled at the dewy morn,
To look, delighted, on the flower just born,
But ere the set of sun at eventide,
The flower was withered, blighted and had died.

So mother's tender boy to manhood grown,
Resists life's storms however fiercely blown,
Till slowly steals the canker to his brain,
And binds his conquered will with powerful
  chain

Forged by that demon, that relentless foe
Of man ; and shrouds that mother's soul in woe.
Death's seal is set upon her idol's brow,
She sinks o'erwhelmed beneath the heavy blow
With broken heart, and heaven's angels come,
And waft her spirit to a brighter home.

O ALCOHOL! thou withering curse of earth,
To untold sorrows hast thou given birth;
Lost souls and blighted homes and lives attest
The crimes committed at thy stern behest.
Behold young Arthur—once the joyous child,
Degraded, demonized, by thee beguiled
To ruin's brink, a wreck in human form,
Dragged to that death "where dieth not the
  worm,"
Where fires unquenchable torment the soul,
Nor gleams one ray of hope while ages roll—
Is dying. Most tormenting agonies
Have seized him. Hear his ravings ere he dies

" Look, see that devil-fish with glaring eyes,
And thousand tentacles ; they slowly rise
And reach for me. O heavens! now I feel
Their slimy coils around me slowly steal
And tighten ; mercy, see that hissing snake
Another, still another; can't I break
This horrid spell which burns my fevered brain,
Consumes my soul with torturing deadly pain ;
O prince of darkness! take me, take me home.
There, see those demons, on they come ; they
  come,
Their eyes like balls of fire, and foot of beast,
And ghoulish appetite on me to feast;
My breath comes hard, oh! let me rest; there,
  see
That other monster comes, he comes for me.
Oh! save me, men, I pray you, beg you save ;
Let not these demons drag me to the grave.
What rises yonder, lurid flame of fire;
Nearer it comes; that sulphurous fume; and
  higher
The smoke ascends.. In letters black as night
One word is written, ' Alcohol;' the blight
Of mother's life. Why speak I now of one—
List! Now I hear her pleading for her son—
A lovely form approaches near me now;
A glittering crown bedecks her angel brow:—
What, vanished; vanished; yes, the vision's
  gone—
Look ; look, behold those serpents coming on,
Damned hissing reptiles; save me from their
  coils.
O Heaven! they have embraced me in their
  toils;
Demons and reptiles, devil-fish and flame ;
Yell, demons, yell, and reptiles hiss my name.
Nearer they come ; and now I feel their breath ;
Oh! welcome monsters, welcome you and
  death.

" A little sleep; what means this drowsy spell?
'Tis growing dark, how strange I feel. Oh! tell
Me, mother, are you here ? Away, away
Black fiend, do let me rest, and pray and pray;
I pray ? too late ; too late, again I say too late,
My everlasting doom is sealed. Sad fate.
'Eternal death;' Oh! let me sleep. How
  weak ;
How parched my lips. O mother! can you
  speak
One word ? She's gone. I'm sinking, sinking
  fast.
A breath or two; the end is come at last ;
Another feeble breath. And is this hell ?
Go monsters, demons, serpents, go and tell,
Go cry aloud and warn earth's drunken host
Of this ' eternal darkness!' I am lost !"

—*L. M. Cunard.*

WHAT THE DIVER SAW.

It was night on the deep, and the dancing wave
  Seemed gemmed with the starry light,
As homeward at last, the brave ship sped,
  Like a bird in her eager flight;
All was slumber below, as the watch, to and fro,
  Trod the deck of his vessel alone,
Or paused for awhile, with a thoughtful smile,
  To listen the night wind's moan.

He thought of the time when his native clime,
  Should greet his return once more,
No longer to toss o'er the treacherous main—
  His toils and his dangers o'er ;
While the sleepers dreamed in their berths beneath,
  Full many a happy dream,—
Of home and their loved ones waiting them there,
  Of cottage and vale and stream.

The morning awoke o'er the tropical isles,
  And glanced o'er the lonely sea ;
But never again on that vessel smiled—
  Nor ever to port came she.
There were anxious groups on the harbor sands,
  That waited and watched in vain ;
But never the lost to their gaze returned
  From over the misty main.

Full many a year, since that sorrowful time,
  Forgotten had rolled away,
When searching for treasure 'neath ocean of Ind,
  A diver went down, one day ;
He traversed the sands of the lonely waste,
  While breakers above him tossed,
Till a rocky reef like a mighty wall,
  His path 'neath the waters crossed.

As nearer he drew to the frowning ledge,
  Lo, there at its shadowy side,
A vessel appeared 'mid the waters dark,
  And swayed in the quiet tide !
The spars and the shrouds of that ghostly bark,
  Loomed forth on his startled eye,
While the tattered shreds of her rotting sails,
  Still hung from her masts on high.

Like a phantom she seemed, in the sombre depths,—
  As solemn and still as a grave ;
And his heart grew still with a sudden thrill,
  For a moment, beneath the wave ;
When at last he climbed to the slimy deck,
  He seemed in a living tomb ;
While the echoes he woke, some horror there spoke—
  Some mystery under the gloom.

Still onward he trod, till he came at last
  To the door of the cabin closed,
Determined to scan, like a fearless man,
  The secrets that there reposed ;
Just then with a groan the door unclosed,
  As slowly the vessel swayed,
While a scene to make e'en a diver quake,
  In a moment was there displayed.

What horrors unthought filled that awful spot!
  Aye, well might he quail in dread ;
For, as waiting him in that crowded space,
  Stood many a score of dead.
There were sturdy men in that drowned throng,
  And others in manly prime ;
There were aged forms with their flowing locks,
  All white with the frosts of time.

There were children, too, with their sunny curls,
  And a smile that was not of earth ;
There were boyish troops and girlish groups
  All missed from many a hearth ;
There were maidens fair, with their streaming hair,
  And beauty still on the cheek ;
Their beseeching eyes still raised to the skies,
  And their lips that seemed to speak.

A moment in terror the diver gazed,
  And they seemed to gaze on him—
Some with glassy stare, some with frenzied glare,
  And others with wan eyes dim ;
Lo! toward him they move—their trample he hears!
  Still nearer they come where he stands ;
He retreats, they pursue ; he fancies he feels
  The clutch of their drowned hands!

At that moment, once more the vessel swayed,
  With a groan closed the cabin door ;
And that ghostly sight, from the diver's view,
  Was hidden forevermore !
Like one half awake from some horrible dream,
  The diver his steps retraced ;
Nor more went he down where the sunken reefs frown,
  To search in their wrecking waste.

Yet ever as life, with its toil and its strife,
  With its sunshine and shadow flees,
That vision is vivid in memory still,
  And that drowned crew he sees ;
Still he fancies a wail of the lost he hears,
  As his hollow footsteps go
O'er the slimy deck of the founded wreck
  That was lost there years ago.
                    —*Horace B. Durant.*

THE HEAVENLY GUEST.

[From the Russian of Count Tolstoi.]

The winter night shuts swiftly down. Within his little humble room
Martin, the good old shoemaker, sits musing in the gathering gloom.
His tiny lamp from off its hook he takes, and lights its friendly beam,
Reaches for his beloved book and reads it by the flickering gleam.

Long pores he o'er the sacred page. At last he lifts his shaggy head.
"If unto me the Master came, how should I welcome Him ?" he said ;
"Should I be like the Pharisee, with selfish thoughts filled to the brim,
Or like the sorrowing sinner—she who weeping ministered to Him ?"

He laid his head upon his arms, and while he thought, upon him crept
Slumber so gentle and so soft he did not realize he slept.
"Martin!" he heard a low voice call. He started, looked toward the door:
No one was there. He dozed again. "Martin!" he heard it call once more.

"Martin, to-morrow I will come. Look out upon the street for me."
He rose and slowly rubbed his eyes, and gazed about him drowsily.
"I dreamed," he said, and went to rest. Waking betimes with morning light,
He wondered, "Were they but a dream, the words I seemed to hear last night ?"

Then, working by his window low, he watched
   the passers-to and fro.
Poor Stephen, feeble, bent, and old, was shoveling
   away the snow;
Martin at last laughed at himself for watching all
   so eagerly.
What fool am I! What look I for? Think I the
   Master's face to see?

"I must be going daft, indeed!" He turned him
   to his work once more.
And stitched awhile, but presently found he was
   watching as before.
Old Stephen leaned against the wall, weary and
   out of breath was he.
"Come in, friend," Martin cried, "come, rest, and
   warm yourself, and have some tea."

"May Christ reward you!" Stephen said, rejoicing
   in the welcome heat;
"I was so tired!" "Sit," Martin begged, "be
   comforted and drink and ent."
But even while his grateful guest refreshed his
   chilled and toil-worn frame
Did Martin's eyes still strive to scan each passing
   form that went and came.

"Are you expecting somebody?" old Stephen
   asked. And Martin told,
Though half ashamed, his last night's dream.
   "Truly, I am not quite so bold
As to expect a thing like that" he said, "yet,
   somehow, still I look!"
With that from off its shelf he took his worn and
   precious Holy Book.

"Yesterday I was reading here, how among sim-
   ple folk He walked
Of old, and taught them. Do you know about it?
   No?" So then he talked
With joy to Stephen. "Jesus said, 'The kind, the
   generous, the poor,
Blessed are they, the humble souls, to be exalted
   evermore'"

With tears of gladness in his eyes poor Stephen
   rose and went his way,
His soul and body comforted; and quietly passed
   on the day,
Till Martin from his window saw a woman shivering in the cold,
Trying to shield her little babe with her thin garment worn and old.

He called her in and fed her, too, and while she
   ate he did his best
To make the tiny baby smile, that she might have
   a little rest;
"Now may Christ bless you, sir!" she cried, when
   warmed and cheered she would have gone;
He took his old cloak from the wall. "'Twill keep
   the cold out. Put it on."

She wept. "Christ led you to look out and pity
   wretched me," said she.
Martin replied, "Indeed He did!" and told his
   story earnestly,
How the low voice said, "I will come," and he had
   watched the livelong day.
"All things are possible," she said, and then she,
   also, went her way.

Once more he sat him down to work, and on the
   passers-by to look.
Till night fell, and then again he lit his lamp and
   took his book.
Another happy hour was spent, when all at once
   he seemed to hear
A rustling sound behind his chair; he listened
   without thought of fear.

He peered about Did something move in yonder
   corner dim and dark?
Was that a voice that spoke his name? "Did you
   not know me, Martin?" "Hark!
Who spoke?" cried Martin. "It is I," replied the
   Voice, and Stephen stepped
Forth from the dusk and smiled at him, and Mar-
   tin's heart within him leapt!

Then, like a cloud was Stephen gone, and once
   again did Martin hear
That heavenly Voice. "And this is I,' sounded
   in tones divinely clear.
From out the darkness softly came the woman
   with the little child,
Gazing at him with gentle eyes, and, as she vanished sweetly smiled.

Then Martin thrilled with solemn joy. Upon the
   sacred page read he:
"Hungry was I, ye gave me meat: thirsty, and ye
   gave drink to me;
A stranger I, ye took me in, and as unto the lowli-
   est one
Of these my brethren, even the least, ye did
   it, unto me 'twas done."

And Martin understood at last it was no vision
   born of sleep,
And all his soul in prayer and praise filled with a
   rapture still and deep.
He had not been deceived, it was no fancy of the
   twilight dim,
But glorious truth! The Master came, and he had
   ministered to Him.
   —*Celia Thaxter, in St. Nicholas.*

THE STAGE-DRIVER'S STORY.

It was the stage-driver's story, as he stood with
   his back to the wheelers,
Quietly flecking his whip and turning his quid of
   tobacco;
While on the dusty road, and blent with the rays
   of the moonlight,
We saw the long curl of his lash and the juice of
   tobacco descending.

"Danger! Sir, I believe you—indeed, I may say
   on that subject,
You your existence might put to the hazard and
   turn of a wager.
I have seen danger? Oh, no! not me, sir, indeed,
   I assure you:
'Twas only the man with the dog that is sitting
   alone in yon wagon.

It was the Geiger Grade, a mile and a half from
   the summit;
Black as your hat was the night, and never a star
   in the heavens.
Thundering down the grade, the gravel and
   stones were sent flying
Over the precipice side—a thousand feet plump
   to the bottom.

Half-way down the grade I felt, sir, a thrilling
   and creaking,
Then a lurch to one side, as we hung on the bank
   of the cannon;
Then, looking up the road, I saw, in the distance
   behind me,
The off hind wheel of the coach just loosed from
   its axle, and following.

t{e glanes at we I gave, that gathered together
my robings,
slanted, and fling them, outspread, on the straining necks of my cattle;
screamed at the top of my voice. and lashed the
air in my frenzy,
While down the Geiger Grade, on three wheels
the vehicle thundered.

Speed was our only chance, when again came the
ominous rattle:
Crack, and another wheel slipped away, and was
lost in the darkness;
Two only now were left; yet such was our fearful
momentum,
Upright. erect, and sustained on two wheels, the
vehicle thundered.

As some huge bowlder, unloosed from its rocky
shelf on the mountain,
Drivers before it the hare and the timorous
squirrel, far leading.
So down the Geiger Grade rushed the pioneer
coach. and before it
Leaped the wild horses, and shrieked in advance
of the danger impending.

But to be brief in my tale. Again, ere we came to
the level,
Slipped from its axle a wheel; so that, to be plain
in my statement,
A matter of twelve hundred yards or more, as the
distance may be,
We traveled upon one wheel, until we drove up to
the station.

Then, sir, we sank in a heap; but picking myself
from the ruins,
I heard a noise up the grade; and looking, I saw
in the distance
The three wheels following still, like moons on
the horizon whirling,
Till, circl'ng, they gracefully sank on the road at
the side of the station.

This is my story, sir; a trifle, indeed, I assure
you;
Much more, perchance, might be said; but I hold
him, of all men, most lightly
Who swerves from the truth in this tale—No,
thank you—well, since you are pressing,
Perhaps I don't care if I do: you may give me the
same, Jim—no sugar."
—*Bret Harte.*

THE MANIAC'S WAIL

I am a wreck, they say; and oft I see
Men gazing in my face all pityingly.
"A wreck!" What can that be? I've stood
apace
Upon the sea shore, when on ocean's face
A frown has rested. and its angry breath
Hath breathed of desolation and of death;
I've seen the vessels. 'mid the tempest's roar,
Tossed like to infants' toys upon the shore
Each crushed, from riven mast to shattered
deck,
And men have cried, "A wreck! a wreck! A
WRECK!

I've trod the forest when across my path
Lay prostrate victims of the tempest's wrath;
And I have heard men murrow when a perated
the giant of the forest long revived
Amidst the fallen; and I've heard them say.
such a wreck ne'er was for many a day
I've seen a costly vase of unpaid worth
Lying in countless fragments on the earth.

And such laments were it were while that day.
You would have thought if had been courted
they.
Over the dying couch I too have sent,
And heard the wailings of a life misspent.
When the wrecked soul sank 'neath despair and
love,
Clutching for mercy's rope. alas, too late!
I am the fated bark!—the smitten tree!—
The shattered vase! Mine the soul's bank-
ruptcy!

*   *   *   *   *   *

Face of seraphic beauty! doomed to be
A light from heav'n, or gleam from hell to me;
Thou break'st in on my solitude e'en now,
But not with glory's halo round thy brow;
Circled with scorching flames! I gasp. I pray.
God! take the horror from my sight away!

*   *   *   *   *   *

In youth I loved. In manhood's strength and
pride
I wooed and won my idol for my bride,
Our home was Eden—Eden, for a snare
Was found therein—a serpent lurked there!
And thus within our home the accursed thing
Lurked, waiting to put forth its adder's sting.
Ere long a whisper came, that on her life
The blight had fallen—my own darling wife!
With wrath I vowed 'twas false ; I cursed the
tongue
That dared against her breathe one word of
wrong.
Yet, with love's heed aroused, my guard I set
Upon her actions. Oh, could I forget
How changed to blackness hopes of rainbow hue,
How soon I proved the words of doom too true!
The record is all darkness, all a blank!
I know not how it was. she slowly sank.
Intemperance! down into thy dark abyss.
My household soon her comely form did miss;
No joy her presence o'er my hearth now shed;
Nay, soon, drink-cursed, she from my bosom
fled!
Wildly I sought her; found her; and. heart-riv'n,
Vowed all should be forgot and all forgiv'n,
If she would but return. And back she came,
Only to fall again; and in her shame
She went in halls of infamy to dwell.
Oh, heavens! to me the thought is worse than
hell!
Mad grew I then; and, lest the world should
see,
With curious eye, a strong man's mis'ry.
I sought a safe retreat, and entered where
Alone my heart could struggle with despair.
I wept until the tears refused to come,
And like a statue stood I. smitten dumb.
My icy heart each melting pow'r defied.
And thus to earth and all therein I died
They brought me here—here, amid wrecks of
mind!
What meeter resting place could ruin find?
I am not fettered. yet wish not to fly
From the poor maniac's discordant cry.
I see no sky. nor hear sweet warbler's sing;
No joy to me do changing season's bring;
For I am dead! For me death's mourning wear!
She dug my grave, and drink entombed me
here!

*   *   *   *   *   *

They bid me upward look—"Up! heav'n is
there!"
And shall I upward look in my despair?
Let them look up who hope. But ne'er to me
Shall hope be given—I care not to be free;

She is not dead,
　But in my heart she lives no more;
Nor shall hope shed
　One ray of light on this dark shore,
I did with fond idolatry adore,
　But love for me apples of Sodom bore!
Sometimes the Drink-fiend comes my way to
　　　　　　　mock,
And when my mind has stemmed the first rude
　　　　　　　shock
Within the past I live again; I glow
With hate; like Samson grappled with my foe!
Till foam upon my parted lips is found,
And the bare walls with frantic shouts resound.
Yea! in my quenchless fury I have prayed
To God, to fiend, both, to grant me their aid,
That trampled 'neath my feet earth's foe might
　　　　　　　lie;
Then have I shouted the rallying cry,
That tells the story of my murdered life—
Dem of hell! Drink fiend!
　　GIVE BACK MY WIFE!!
　　　　　　　—*Harriet A. Glazebrook.*

JOHN DARRYLL'S DREAM.

ONE day, as he strolled down the village street,
John Darryll chanced an old friend to meet.

"How are you, old boy?" was the greeting
　warm,
"Come in for an hour, out of the storm,

And we'll have a chat and a smoke together,
And a drink to offset this wild March weather."

And he linked his arm in John's, and led
The boy's feet on toward a sign ahead,

Where "Wines and Liquors," in great gold let-
　ters,
Linked together like demon's fetters.

Told the passers-by that within was sold
Sorrow, and ruin, and shame untold.

They crossed the threshold and entered in
Where never before the lad had been.

Warm and pleasant, and fair to see,
This starting-place to misery.

"Something to drink," the boy's friend said,
And John walked up to the bar with dread.

But he dared not say, as he knew he ought,
A firm, strong "No." "Just this once," he
　thought.

He drank the draught that his friend held out—
His first and his last beyond a doubt!

Ah! little, how little, we think or know
Of the easy path that leads down so low.

One step—and the others come fast and free—
And before we know it comes misery.

Then he and his friend sat down to chat
Of old school-day friends, and this, and that.

It seemed to John that a wizard's spell
On him and those about him fell.

The present vanished. The future was here.
He had lived, in a moment, full many a year.

He stood in a room that was cold and bare,
And a man was alone in the shadows there.

A man with a face like his, but old
In a life whose shame can not be told.

Old in shame, but still young in years,
A fitting sight for an angel's tears.

John Darryll looked on the wreck and c[...]:
"This man is myself! Would God I had c[...]

"Before the fetters were forged on me
That bind my soul eternally.

"I must die like a dog and be forgot,
Save by the few who could help me not.

"A drunkard! May god forgive me the woe
I have caused the mother who loved me so!"

He woke from his dream with a sob and moan
And found himself on the street alone.

"Thank God, it was *only* a dream!" cried he,
"God in His mercy sent it to me.

"To warn me of danger. Never again
Shall the draught that is ruin to souls of men

"Pass these lips of mine." An old man now,
John Darryll remembers and keeps his vow,
　　　　　　　—*Eben E. Rexford.*

THE FIREMAN.

THE city slumbers. O'er its mighty walls
Night's dusky mantle soft and silent falls;
Sleep o'er the world slow waves its wand of lead,
And ready torpors wrap each sinking head.
Stilled is the stir of labor and of life;
Hushed is the hum, and tranquilized the strife.
Man is at rest with all his hopes and fears;
The young forget their sports, the old their cares;
The grave are careless; those who joy or weep,
All rest contented on the arm of sleep.

Sweet is the pillowed rest of beauty now,
And slumber smiles upon her tranquil brow,
Her bright dreams lead her to the moonlit tide,
Her heart's own partner wandering by her side.
'Tis a summer eve; the soft gales scarcely rouse
The low-voiced ripple and the rustling boughs;
And faint and far, some minstrel's melting tone
Breathes to her heart a music like its own.

When, hark! Oh, horror! What a crash is there!
What shriek is that which fills the midnight air?
'Tis "FIRE! FIRE!" She wakes to dream no
　more!
The hot blast rushes through the blazing door!
The dim smoke eddies round; and hark! that cry!
"HELP! HELP! *Will no one aid? I die—I die!*"
She seeks the casement; shuddering at its height,
She turns again; the fierce flames mock her flight;
Along the crackling stairs they fiercely play,
And roar exulting, as they seize their prey.
"*Help!* HELP! Will no one come!" She says no
　more,
But, pale and breathless, sinks upon the floor.

Will no one save thee? Yes, there yet is one
Remains to save when hope itself is gone;
When all have fled—when all but he would fly,
The *fireman* comes to rescue or to die!
He mounts the stair—it wavers 'neath his tread;
He seeks the room—flames flashing round his
　head;
He bursts the door, he lifts her prostrate frame,
And turns again to brave the raging flame.

The fire-blast smites him with its stifling breath,
The fallen timbers menace him with death,
The sinking floors his hurried steps betray,
And ruin crashes round his desperate way;
Hot smoke obscures—ten thousand cinders rise—
Yet still he staggers forward with his prize.
He leaps from burning stair to stair. On! On!
Courage! One effort more, and all is won!

THE OLD PARSON'S STORY.

They say I am old an' feeble;
My eyes ez as dim ez a mole;
My shoulders are all out a kilter;
My mind ez beginnin' to fail:
They want a much younger preacher,
More full of forgiveness an' love,
To talk to 'em here about providence,
An' more of the masters above.

For fifty long years I've been preachin',
I've studied my old Bible well;
I know how fair it my duty
To draw 'em the horrors o' hell.
Perhaps I've been wrong in my notions;
I've follered the scriptur's, I know,
An' never her knowin'ly broken
The vows that I took long ago.

I've seen many trials an' changes;
I've hed a good fight against wrong;
The gals hev grown up to be women,
The boys hev cum manly an' strong.
The homes old deacons hev vanished,
Their peace Eves hev come to a close;
They sleep in the silent old churchyard,
Where soon I shall lie in repose.

My back hez been alwus complainin'
The church wuz not rightly arranged;
They voted to hev a high steeple,
The gallery had to be changed.
They built up a fanciful rostry,
They bought the bees organ to play;
They changed the old pews into kindlin's,
And tumbled the tall pulpit down.

And now, as my pate an' my sorrer,
They say "The old parson must go,"
I know I am childish an' feeble,
My steps are unsteady an' slow;
They want a more spirited speaker,
With modern ideas in his head,
To induce round the plot form an' holler,
And wake up the souls that are dead.

I'll try to believe that what happens
Will always come out for the best.
They tell me my labor is ended,
The time I was taking a rest.
I've been o' comfort an' riches,
I'm satisfied my conscience is clear,
An' when in the churchyard I'm sleepin'
Perhaps they may wish I was here.

TWO LIVES AND A LIFE.

Founded on the drama of that name by Messrs.
Tom Taylor and Chas. Reade.

To the scaffold's foot she came;
Looked her blank eyes into shame,
Hate and foll her griefing breast,
There a pardon calmly pressed.

She had heard her lover's doom—
Heard the price upon his head,
" I will save him," she had said

" Betrayed Annie loves him too,
She will weep, but Ruth will do;
Who should save him, and disgraced,
Who can slay who loves him most."

To the scaffold now she came,
I'm her first hope past his name,—
Ruth, and fel a closer died,—
I now verified by his side.

Over Annie's face he bent,
Raised her wild face Annie's tomb
"'Tis," he called her—called her "wife!"
Simple word to cure a life!

In Ruth's breast the passion lay,
But she coldly turned away—
" He has scaled his traitor fate,
I can love, and I can hate "

" Annie is his wife," they said
" Be it wife, then, to the dead,
Since the dying she will mate;
I can love, and I can hate;"

" What their sin?   They do but love,
Let this thought thy bosom move."
Came the jealous answer straight,—
" I can love, and I can hate!"

" Mercy!" still they cried. But she:
" Who has mercy open me?
Who? My life is desolate—
I can love, and I can hate!"

From the scaffold steps she went,
Shouts the murder silence rent,—
All the air was quick with cries,—
" See the traitor! see, he dies!"

Back she looked with stifled scream,
Saw the axe a-swinging gleam;
All her woman's anger died,—
" From the king?" she madly cried—

" From the king. His name—behold!"
Quick the parchment she unrolled,
Passed the axe in upward swing—
" He is pardoned!   Live the king!"

Glad the cry, and loud and long;
All about the scaffold throng,—
There entwining fold in fold,
Raven tresses, Rocks of gold.

There against Ruth's tortured breast
Annie's tearful face is pressed.
While the white lips murmuring move—
" I can hate—but I can love!"
—William Sawyer.

CRIPPLE BEN.

Down in a street by the river's side,
Where ebbs and flows the hurrying tide
Of city life, in a squalid den,
Hungry and poor dwelt " Cripple Ben."
So they called him; no other name
He e'er had boasted since first he came.
Unknown, unnoticed, his care to hide.
In that wretched home by the river's side.
Ragged, one-legged, deformed was he;
His age not over twenty-and-three.
All day long on his crutch he'd go
Through the streets with a painful gait and slow,
Vending matches and pins, and soap
Ever cheery and full of hope,
Never complaining, never sad,
With an eye so bright, and a face so glad,
In spite of his cares, that folks would pause
In passing, to buy from his little stores;
And children would see his cheerful smile
Reflected back in their own the while.
And even the rough, blunt, sailor-men
Had always a word for " Cripple Ben."
Yet oft on the pier where his great crutch lay,
He'd sit and rest on a summer's day,
And gazing o'er the green-grown brink
On the swirling tide below, would think

And wonder if in yon current there
He could bury forever his weight of care.
" Nobody cares for me," he'd say ;
" I'm weary of toiling every day.
By night a hard and narrow bed,
By day a beggarly crust of bread.
Why not finish it all ? And then
Nobody 'll miss poor Cripple Ben."
Yet something within him said: "Live on ;
Though thy heart be lonely, thy features wan,
Even for thee its rests in store
To do some good ere thy life is o'er."
So then, with a sigh of silent pain,
He'd hobble away on his crutch again.
And take up his burden of life once more,
Bravely and patiently as before.
One day last June, in an eager hunt
For a friend's place, down by the river front,
I suddenly heard a piercing a cry,
A cry of grief from the pier hard
And half a hundred hurrying feet
Were speeding across the rough-paved street.
I joined the crowd. At the pier-head, lo!
A woman wringing her hands in woe,
Screamed, "Oh! my child!" while men did shout,
And out in the current, out, far out,
A man was struggling to keep afloat
A baby form. "A boat! a boat!"
We shouted. Then stalwart arms and brave
Pulled hurriedly forth, two lives to save.
'Twas not in vain, for quicker than thought,
Those dripping two to the pier they brought.
" The child's alive! ' they cried with zest,
And the babe was clasped to its mother's breast.
But what of him—the other one—
With his face upturned to the noonday sun ?
Lifeless they lifted him up, and then
A bystander said: "*Why it's Cripple Ben !* "
—*George L. Catlin.*

THE "DEADMAN'S JOURNEY."

HARK! my hardy mates of the camp-fire side,
Till I tell you the way Josh Murphy died.
You knew him well—a comrade true
As e'er pulled trigger or lasso threw ;
Like a child in peace, but in battle bold,
With a hand of steel and a heart of gold ;
A hundred times it was mine to ride
On the dangerous scout by Josh's side ;
And so I rode on the dreadful night
When his gallant spirit took its flight.

It was the spring of sixty-four,
Just a little while ere the war was o'er,
That 'twas mine the mail-bags to transport
From Stevenson Post to Totten Fort ;
Through the rugged passes the route to take
O'er the mountains that frown on " Devil's Lake;"
Those canyons alive with the skulking crews.
Of the Chippewas and the savage Sioux ;
But my heart felt light and my arm felt strong,
For brave Josh Murphy rode along.

So in lightsome trim, we dashed away
Till Steve'son dim in the distance lay ;
And we climbed on the mountains' rugged heads
Keeping wary watch for the wily reds.
Till the sun swept down the western blue,
And we saw Fort Totten spring to view.
We could note how the breeze-blown cedars
    swayed
O'er the eight-foot crest of the grim stockade,
And we caught, by the aid that the field-glass
    lent,
The sun-flash on arm and accoutrement,
As lovers and husbands thronged the gate,
With brightened glances and hearts-elate.
To see us pictured against the sky,
O'er the highest range where the mail-routes lie.
And we seemed to hear the joyous hail
That welcomed the sight of the longed-for mail.

But soon we were lost to their eager gaze
In the darkening depths of the canyon's maze,
And thoughts of rest—all danger gone—
Cheered our weary paths as we journeyed on,
Till, deep in the gorge, Josh Murphy stopped,
"Ho, Charlie," he cried, "there's a mail-bag
    dropp'd."

Right smart at the word, I sprang to the ground
And hurried back till the bag was found ;
As I stooped to lift it, a dreadful yell
Split the mountain air like a shriek from hell,
And I saw poor Josh from his saddle slide,
And sink in blood by his pony's side.
My Spencer unslung, I hurried back
'Mid showering shot and rifle's crack,
And the taunting jeer and the maddening mocks
Of the ambushed fiends 'mid the shattered rocks.

I bent over Josh in the deepest despair,
As he stroked his long, red, clustering hair—
" You scalp me, Charlie ! " he faintly said,
" Don't leave my hair to a cursed red,
And bear to the camp one blood-stained curl,
To be worn on the heart of my little girl."
Then I bawled in his ear through the horrid din ;
" By Heaven's help, Josh, I will take you in !"

And Heaven did aid our desperate flight
With the friendly cloak of a pitch dark night.
To his saddle I raised his fainting form.
And we struggled away through the leaden
    storm ;
And Josh, with his face on his pony's mane,
Was madly borne to the open plain.
That livelong night o'er the dark expanse,
I wandered about in a sort of trance.
Loudly I called on my comrade's name,
But no answering sound from the blackness
    came.
And down in the prairie grass I lay
To wait for the dawn of the tardy day.
And I thought as the east began to glow,
That I heard the sound of the charging foe,
When upon the scene, like a thunder-burst,
Dashed the gallant boys of the Thirty-first.
With warm embrace and grasp of hand,
I was gladly hailed by the warrior band.
We sought for Josh and we struck his trail,
In the dew-damp notes of the scattered mail ;
And we found him at last scarce a pistol-shot
From the picket wall of the fort he'd sought ;
There he proudly lay with his unscalped head
On the throbless breast of his pony—dead—
And the route from the pass to that cedared hill
Is known as " THE DEADMAN'S JOURNEY," still.

This poem is founded on fact. The localities,
the mission, the names, and the catastrophe are
all true.

FAITHFUL.

A LONG, bare ward in the hospital;
    A dying girl in the narrow bed ;
A nurse, whose footsteps lightly fall,
    Soothing softly that restless head.

Slain by the man she learned to love,
    Beaten, murdered and flung away ;
None beheld it but God above,
    And she who bore it. And there she lay.

" A little drink of water, dear ? "
    Slowly the white lips gasp and sip.
" Let me turn you over, so you can hear,
    While I let the ice on your temple drip."

A look of terror disturbs her face;
Firm and silent those pale lips close;
A stranger stands in the nurse's place;
"Tell us who hurt you, for no one knows.

A glitter of joy is in her eye;
Faintly she whispers; "Nobody did,"
And one tear christens the loving lie
From the heart in that wounded bosom hid.

"Nobody did it!" she says again,
"Nobody hurt me!" Her eyes grew dim;
But in the spasm of mortal pain,
She says to herself: "I've saved you, Jim!"

Day by day, as the end draws near,
To gentle question or stern demand,
Only that one response they hear,
Though she lifts to Heaven her wasted hand.

"Nobody hurt me!" They see her die,
The same words still on her latest breath;
With a tranquil smile she tells her lie,
And glad goes down to the gates of death

Beaten, murdered, but faithful still,
Loving above all wrong and woe,
If she has gone to a world of ill,
Where, oh! saint, shall we others go?

Even, I think that evil man
Has hope of a better life in him,
When she so loved him her last words ran:
"Nobody hurt me! I've saved you, Jim!"
          —*Rose Terry Cooke.*

SOMEBODY'S DARLING.

INTO a ward of unwhitewashed walls,
Where the dead and dying lay—
Wounded by bayonets, shells, and balls—
Somebody's Darling was borne one day.
Somebody's Darling! So young and so brave,
Wearing still on his pale, sweet face,
Soon to be hid by the dust of the grave,
The lingering light of his boyhood's grace.

Matted and damp are the curls of gold
Kissing the snow of that fair young brow,
Pale are the lips of delicate mould—
Somebody's Darling is dying now!
Back from the beautiful blue-veined face
Brush every wandering silken thread;
Cross his hands as a sign of grace—
Somebody's Darling is still and dead!

Kiss him once for somebody's sake;
Murmur a prayer, soft and low;
One bright curl from the cluster take—
They were somebody's pride, you know.
Somebody's hand had rested there;
Was it a mother's, soft and white?
And have the lips of a sister fair
Been baptized in those waves of light?

God knows best! He was somebody's love;
Somebody's heart enshrined him there;
Somebody wafted his name above.
Night and morn, on the wings of prayer;
Somebody wept when he marched away,
Looking so handsome, brave, and grand;
Somebody's kiss on his forehead lay;
Somebody clung to his parting hand.

Somebody's watching and waiting for him,
Yearning to hold him again to her heart;
There he lies—with his blue eyes dim,
And smiling, childlike lips apart,
Tenderly bury the fair young dead,
Pausing to drop on his grave a tear;
Carve on the wooden slab at his head,
"Somebody's Darling lies buried here!"

KATE SHELLY.

HAVE you heard how a girl saved the lightning
express,—
Of Kate Shelly, whose father was killed on the
road?
Were he living to-day, he'd be proud to possess
Such a daughter as Kate Ah! 'twas grit that
she showed
On that terrible evening when Donahue's train
Jumped the bridge and went down, in the dark-
ness and rain.

She was only eighteen, but a woman in size,
With a figure as graceful and lithe as a doe;
With peach-blossom cheeks, and with violet eyes.
And teeth and complexion like new-fallen snow;
With a nature unspoiled and unblemished by art,
With a generous soul, and a warm, noble heart

'Tis evening—the darkness is dense and profoun'
Men linger at home by their bright-blazing fir
The wind wildly howls with a horrible sound,
And shrieks through the vibrating telegra
wires;
The fierce lightning flashes along the dark sky;
The rain falls in torrents; the river rolls by.

The scream of a whistle! the rush of a train!
The sound of a bell! a mysterious light
That flashes and flares through the fast-fallin
rain!
A rumble! a roar! shrieks of human affright!
The falling of timbers! the space of a breath!
A splash in the river! then darkness and death!

Kate Shelly recoils at the terrible crash!
The sounds of destruction she happens to hear
She springs to the window—she throws up th
sash,
And listens and looks with a feeling of fear
The tall tree-tops groan, and she hears the faint cr
Of a drowning man down in the river near by!

Her heart feebly flutters, her features grow wan,
And then through her soul in a moment ther
flies
A forethought that gives her the strength of
man—
She turns to her trembling old mother and cries
"I must save the express—'twill be here in a
hour!"
Then out through the door disappears in th
shower.

She flies down the track through the pitiless rai
She reaches the river—the water below
Whirls and seethes through the timbers. Sh
shudder's again:
"The bridge! To Moingona God help me to go!
Then closely about her she gathers her gown
And on the wet ties with a shiver sinks down.

Then carefully over the timbers she creeps
On her hands and her knees, almost holding her
breath.
The loud thunder peals and the wind wildly
sweeps,
And struggles to hurry her downward to death;
But the thought of the train to destruction so near
Removes from her soul every feeling of fear.

With the blood dripping down from each torn'
bleeding limb,
Slowly over the timbers her dark way she feels;
Her fingers grow numb and her head seems to
swim;
Her strength is fast failing—she staggers' she
reels!
She falls——Ah! the danger is over at last,
Her feet touch the earth, and the long bridge is
passed!

In an instant new life seems to come to her form ;
   She springs to her feet and forgets her despair.
On, on to Moingona! She faces the storm,
   She reaches the station—the keeper is there.
" Save the lightning-express! No—hang out the
   red light!
There's death on the bridge at the river to-night!"

Out flashes the signal-light, rosy and red ;
   Then sounds the loud roar of the swift coming
    train,
The hissing of steam, and there, brightly ahead,
   The gleam of a headlight illumines the rain.
' Down brakes!" shrieks the whistle, defiant and
   shrill ;
She heeds the red signal—she slackens, she's still!

Ah! noble Kate Shelly, your mission is done ;
   Your deed that dark night will not fade from
    our gaze ;
An endless renown you have worthily won :
   Let the nation be just, and accord you its praise.
Let your name, let your fame, and your courage
   declare
What a *woman* can do, and a *woman* can dare!
   —*Eugene J. Hall, in Harper's Young People.*

THE OLD SERGEANT.

" COME a little nearer, Doctor!—thank you—let me
   take the cup;
Draw your chair up—draw it closer—just another
   little sup!
Maybe you may think I'm better: but I'm pretty
   well used up—
Doctor, you've done all you could do, but I'm just
   a-going up!

" Feel my pulse, sir! if you want to, but it ain't
   much use to try "—
" Never say that! " said the surgeon, as he smoth-
   er'd down a sigh :
" It will never do, old comrade! for a soldier to
   say die!"
" What you say will make no difference, Doctor!
   when you come to die.

" Doctor! what has been the matter?" " You
   were very faint, they say.
You must try to get to sleep now."—" Doctor!
   have I been away ?"
" Not that anybody knows of!"—" Doctor—
   Doctor! please to stay!
There is something I must tell you, and you wont
   have long to stay!

" I have got my marching orders, and I'm ready
   now to go;
Doctor, did you say I fainted ?—but it couldn't ha'
   been so,—
For as sure as I'm a sergeant, and was wounded
   at Shiloh,
I've this very night been back there, on the old
   field of Shiloh !

" This is all that I remember—The last time the
   Lighter came,
And the lights had all been lower'd, and the
   noises much the same.
He had not been gone five minutes before some-
   think call'd my name :
' Orderly Sergeant—Robert Burton!'—just that
   way it call'd my name.

" And I wonder'd who could call me so distinctly
   and so slow,—
Knew it couldn't be the Lighter,—he could not
   have spoken so,—
And I tried to answer—' Here, sir !' but I couldn't
   make it go:
For I couldn't move a muscle, and I couldn't make
   it go!

" Then I thought: It's all nightmare, all a hum-
   bug and a bore ;
Just another foolish *grape-vine*—and it wont come
   any more ;
But it came, sir! notwithstanding, just the same
   way as before:
' Orderly Sergeant—Robert Burton!'—even plainer
   than before.

" That is all that I remember, till a sudden burst
   of light,
And I stood beside the river, where we stood that
   Sunday night,
Waiting to be ferried over to the dark bluffs op-
   posite,
When the river was perdition, and all hell was op-
   posite!

" And the same old palpitation came again in all
   its power,
And I heard a bugle sounding as from some celes-
   tial tower :
And the same mysterious voice said: ' It is the
   eleventh hour!
Orderly Sergeant—Robert Burton—It is the
   eleventh hour!'

" Doctor Austin!—what day is this ?"—" It is
   Wednesday night, you know."—
" Yes! to-morrow will be New Year's, and a right
   good time below!
What time is it, Doctor Austin?"—" Nearly
   twelve."—" Then don't you go!
Can it be that all this happened—all this—not an
   hour ago!

" There was where the gunboats open'd on the
   dark rebellious host ;
And where Webster semicircled his last guns upon
   the coast,
There were still the two log-houses, just the same,
   or else their ghost,—
And the same old transport came and took me
   over—or its ghost !

" And the old field lay before me, all deserted far
   and wide;
There was where they fell on Prentiss,—there
   M'Clernand met the tide ;
There was where stern Sherman rallied, and
   where Hurlbut's heroes died—
Lower down, where Wallace charged them, and
   kept charging till he died.

" There was where Lew Wallace show'd them he
   was of the canny kin,
There was where old Nelson thunder'd, and where
   Rousseau waded in ;
There M'Cook sent 'em to breakfast, and we all
   began to win—
There was where the grape-shot took me, just as
   we began to win.

" Now a shroud of snow and silence over every
   thing was spread,
And but for this old blue mantle, and the old hat
   on my head,

i should not have even doubted, to this moment, I
    was dead,—
For my footsteps were as silent as the snow upon
    the dead!

" Death and silence!—Death and silence, all
    around me as I sped!
And behold a mighty Tower, as is builded to the
    dead,—
To the Heaven of the heavens, lifted up its mighty
    head,
Till the Stars and Stripes of Heaven all seem'd
    waving from its head!

" Round and mighty-based it tower'd—up into the
    infinite—
And I knew no mortal mason could have built a
    shaft so bright;
For it shone like solid sunshine; and a winding
    stair of light
Wound around it and around it till it wound clear
    out of sight!

" And behold, as I approach'd it—with a rapt and
    dazzled stare,—
Thinking that I saw old comrades just ascending
    the great Stair,—
Suddenly the solemn challenge broke of—' Halt!
    and who goes there!'
'I'm a friend,' I said, 'if you are.' 'Then ad-
    vance, sir, to the Stair!'

" I advanced!—That sentry, Doctor! was Elijah
    Ballantyne!—
First of all to fall on Monday, after we had form'd
    the line!—
' Welcome, my old Sergeant! welcome! Welcome
    by that countersign!'
And he pointed to the scar there, under this old
    cloak of mine!

" As he grasp'd my hand I shudder'd, thinking
    only of the grave;
But he smiled and pointed upward with a bright
    and bloodless glaive;
' That's the way, sir! to Headquarters.'—' What
    Headquarters?'—' of the Brave.'—
' By the great Tower!'—' That '—he answer'd—' is
    the way, sir! of the Brave!'—

" Then a sudden shame came o'er me at his uni-
    form of light;
At my own so old and tatter'd, and at his so new
    and bright;
' Ah!' said he—'you have forgotten the New Uni-
    form to-night,
Hurry back, for you must be here at just twelve
    o'clock to-night!'

" And the next thing I remember, you were sitting
    there, and I—
Doctor, did you hear a footstep? Hark!—God
    bless you all! Good-bye!
Doctor! please to give my musket and my knap-
    sack, when I die,
To my son—my son that's coming—he won't get
    here till I die!

" Tell him his old father bless'd him as he never
    did before—
And to carry that old musket—Hark! a knock is
    at the door!—
Till the Union—See! it opens!" "Father! Father!
    speak once more!—"
" Bless you!" gasped the old gray Sergeant, and
    he lay and said no more!
        —*Byron Forceythe Wilson.*

ROVING NED.

DIVORCED, did they say? What! I. Roving Ned
Divorced in disgrace from the woman I wed
In the wealth of her beauty, five summers to-night,
'Mid the chiming of bells and happiness bright!
O, God, can it be? Have I fallen so low?
Divorced from that bride—and I loved her so °

Was that Eden a dream? Was that husband's first
    kiss
But an apple of Sodom in the feast of my bliss?
Were those vows that I spoke but the words of
    untruth—
A perjurer's lie to the love of his youth?
Were those visions I saw but a mirage of fate
And the words of endearment the seeds of a hate?

Was that life in the cottage a dream of the past?
And the joy that it brought us too precious to
    last?
Did the child that was sent us return in its flight
To escape the dark shadows now clouding this
    night?
Were our hopes, then so bright, to be shrouded in
    gloom,
And the roses so sweet but the bloom of the tomb?

Bound helpless in sin! Ah, I see it now plain,
And thou, damning glass, hath enwoven the
    chain!
O, sparkle and gleam, but I know thee too well;
Thy diamonds of joy are the jewels of hell.
The wealth of thy pleasure is sorrow and care
And the spell of thy charm but the gall of despair.

Ah, sparkle and glimmer, I see in thy tide
The hand that was raised to a once worshiped
    bride.
Ah, sparkle and glitter! I see a dread flight
From a drunkard enraged through a cold winter's
    night.
That husband so proud but a wreck is now left,
Of love and affection and manhood bereft.

I see a lone wanderer over the earth,
Now shunned and disowned by the kin of his
    birth,
So weary of life, but too sinful to die,
With the pangs of remorse 'neath the frowns from
    on high,
Far downward he sinks till his oaths sound the
    knell
Of a soul that is tottering on the verge of a hell.

Cursed be thee, glass! Is thy conquest complete?
No! I will grind thee, fiend, yet 'neath my feet'
By a mother's last prayer, by the home of my
    birth,
I will dash thee in fragments down swift to the
    earth!
By the love of that woman that once my name
    bore
I will rise from a slave to my manhood once more.

Come, friends of my youth, there's a soul to be
    saved.
Give me of thy strength, there are storms to be
    braved.
Come back, O my will, with all of thy might
And make me a giant to battle for right.
To Earth and to Heaven again I will call
And snatch even life from the folds of a pall.

God help me to stand by the vows that I make;
God help me, if any, in weakness I break;
Lead me not to the tempter but guide me in right
Until I am strong in thy mercy and might
Then lead back my bride to her husband again
And link with thy blessing the now parted chain.
        —*Sherman D. Richardson.*

SMITING THE ROCK.

The stern old judge, in relentless mood,
Glanced at the two who before him stood ;
She was bowed and haggard and old,
He was young and defiant and bold,—
Mother and son ; and to gaze at the pair,
Their different attitudes, look and air,
One would believe, ere the truth were known,
The mother convicted and not the son.

There was the mother ; the boy stood nigh
With a shameless look, and his head held high.
Age had come over her, sorrow and care ;
These mattered but little so he was there,
A prop to her years and a light to her eyes,
And prized as only a mother can prize ;
But what for him could a mother say,
Waiting his doom on a sentence day.

Her husband had died in his shame and sin ;
And she a widow, her living to win,
Had toiled and struggled from morn till night,
Making with want a wearisome fight,
Bent over her work with resolute zeal,
Till she felt her old frame totter and reel,
Her weak limbs tremble, her eyes grow dim !
But she had her boy, and she toiled for him.

And he,—he stood in the criminal dock,
With a heart as hard as a flinty rock,
An impudent glance and a reckless air,
Braving the scorn of the gazers there ;
Dipped in crime and encompassed round
With proof of his guilt by captors found,
Ready to stand, as he phrased it, " game,"
Holding not crime but penitence, shame.

Poured in a flood o'er the mother's cheek
The moistening prayers where the tongue was
  weak,
And she saw through the mist of those bitter tears
Only the child in his innocent years ;
She remembered him pure as a child might be,
The guilt of the present she could not see ;
And for mercy her wistful looks made prayer
To the stern old judge in his cushioned chair.

" Woman," the old judge steadily said—
" Your boy is the neighborhood's plague and dread ;
Of a gang of reprobates chosen chief ;
An idler and rioter, ruffian and thief.
The jury did right, for the facts were plain ;
Denial is idle, excuses are vain.
The sentence the court imposes is one—"
" Your honor," she cried, " he's my only son."

The constables grinned at the words she spoke,
And a ripple of fun through the court-room broke ;
But over the face of the culprit came
An angry look and a shadow of shame ;
" Don't laugh at my mother !" loud cries he ;
" You've got me fast, and can deal with me ;
But she's too good 'or your coward jeers,
And I'll—" then h\ utterance choked with tears.

The judge for a moment bent his head,
And looked at him keenly, and then he said :
" We suspend the sentence,—the boy can go ; "
And the words were tremulous, forced and low,
" But say !" and he raised his finger then—
" Don't let them bring you hither again.
There is something good in you yet, I know ;
I'll give you a chance—make the most of it—Go ! "

The twain went forth, and the old judge said ;
" I meant to have given him a year instead.
And perhaps 'tis a difficult thing to tell,
If clemency here be ill or well.
But a rock was struck in that callous heart,
From which a fountain of good may start ;
For one on the ocean of crime long tossed,
Who loves his mother is not quite lost."

A KEEPER'S STORY.

" Stark mad, sir ! A wild, wolfish beast
  Is this Hugh. Did you happen to hear
Of his crime ? It was done at Chadd's Ford,
  Chester county, nigh this time last year.
No ? Well, sir, it was this way. Of course
  It began with a girl—Kitty Roe—
As pretty a lass as e'er stepped
  To her own happy songs to and fro.

" In garden, in dairy, in kirk,
  She was fair as a blossom to meet,
Her hair like a new chestnut shone,
  Her cheek shamed the June roses sweet.
Lovers ? Bless you, a score, I'm sure,
  All bewitched with her beauty ! Perhaps
She might have coquetted. In time
  The list narrowed down to two chaps.

" One, handsome Joe Blaine, a farm-hand ;
  Strong and straight as a sapling was Joe ;
Wind-brown 'twixt the beard and the eyes,
  But his forehead was white as the snow ;
His hair glittered gold in the sun,
  And his laugh was a pleasure to hear—
Alas ! I say ' was !' How it rang
  Through the glad closing days of last year !

" The other, this fellow you see
  In the cell ; he was called Fighting Hugh.
He tended the draw at the bridge,
  Where a schooner now and then came
    through ;
A fist like a hammer, a voice
  Rough and deep like a lion's. They say
Kitty smiled on his suit awhile
  Just to tease faithful Joe (a girl's way) ;

" And so came one fair Sabbath morn
  Bright and beautiful, just as if sin
Had fled from the world. Nothing jarred,
  No train smote the ear with its din.
A promise Kate gave over night—
  'Twas to ride on a hand-car with Joe—
The lasses and lads often sped
  On their holiday journeying so.

" Joe draped her a seat like a throne,
  Where she sat a young queen, gay and fair.
Her scarlet shawl folded about,
  A snowy scarf tied o'er her hair.
Joe's strong arms the stout handles whirled,
  Till the grade sent them swiftly along,
Quite fearless, nor vessel nor train
  Thrilled a fear in the heart of their song.

" How the curve of the twin rails shone
  Far away down the line of the road ;
How the car with its fair, glad freight
  In the sun softly glittering glowed,
So neared they Fox River. The light
  Of its waters danced gay in the sun ;
As they rounded the curve so fast
  All the milestones seemed blurred into one.

" ' God save us, the draw !' shrieked the girl.
  ' Look !' The twain straight ahead saw their
    fate—
The draw was wide open ! and Hugh,
  With his arms folded, watching them sate.

*   *   *   *   *   *

" They found them, dead, lying beneath
  The rough, ragged rock by the mill,
Clasped close to each other in death,
  Wed by ritual solemn and still.

" A maniac lingers dark Hugh,
  Seeing always that vision go by,
Facing always his fearful sin,
  Hearing always poor Kitty's last cry."
              —*Ethel Rynn.*

THE CROSSING OF THE BRIDGE.

HAVE you ever heard the story
  How Tim Nesbitt crossed the bridge?
When the down express came roaring
  Round the curves of Smoky Ridge?

You remember the big trestle
  Just this side of Carey's mill;
Twenty miles about from Sharon,
  And as far from Smoky Hill?

Half a mile in length—they say so—
  And it's not a yard-stick less—
Fifty feet above the creek, too;
  That's as near as I can guess.

And just as Tim came round the curve
  And saw the bridge ahead,
He felt the track was giving, like,
  And knew the rails had spread.

Down grade at that, and thirty miles—
  That was her common run—
A bridge not fifty yards ahead,
  Oh Heaven! what could be done!

Like jangling millstones bounced the cars
  Along the sleepers' ends;
Tim had no time to think of wife,
  Of babe, or self, or friends.

The fireman jumped, but quick as thought
  Tim Nesbitt took it in—
The bridge is straight, there is a chance
  For life if he should win.

And with a mighty jerk he threw
  The throttle open wide—
And said a prayer—and "Lady Bess"
  Went on her crazy ride.

Dreadful! You might have seen the wood
  And nails, and glasses fly,
And splinters, torn from bridge and beam,
  And clamps from every tie.

While "Lady Bess" just flew across,
  And Tim just held his breath—
While half the passengers had swooned,
  And half were sure of death.

But ere the scared had time to pray,
  Or broken wheels to stand,
Tim Nesbitt's train had crossed the bridge,
  And we were safe on land.

I reckon that no other man
  That runs upon the line,
Has got a watch as big as his,
  Nor anything so fine.

For on one side's a picture like
  The creek at Smoky Ridge—
And on the other's writ: "To him
  Who run across the bridge."
                    —*S. H. M. Byers.*

THE LIFE BRIGADE.

WILD are the mountainous billows
  That break on the rocky shore,
Wildly whistles the storm-wind
  Through crevice, window, and door
Down in relentless fury
  Falls a torrent of icy rain,
And, back with its wrath, the tempest
  Rides over the rolling main.

Hark! 'mid the strife of waters
  A shrill despairing cry,
As of some drowning sailor
  In his last agony!
Another! and now are mingled
  Heart-rending shrieks for aid.
Lo! a sinking ship. What ho! arouse,
  Arouse the Life Brigade!

They come with hurrying footsteps:
  No need for a second call;
They are broad awake and ready,
  And willing one and all.
Not a hand among them trembles,
  Each tread is firm and free,
Not one man's spirit falters
  In the face of the awful sea.

Yet well may the bravest sailor
  Shrink back appalled to-night
From that army of massive breakers
  With their foam-crests gleaming white
Those beautiful, terrible breakers,
  Waiting to snatch their prey,
And bury yon hapless vessel
  'Neath a monument of spray!

But rugged, and strong, and cheery
  Dauntless and undismayed,
Are the weather-beaten heroes
  Of the gallant Life Brigade.
"To the rescue!" shouts their leader,
  Nor pauses for reply—
A plunge!—and the great waves bear him
  Away to do or die!

The whole night long, unwearied,
  They battle with wind and sea,
All ignorant and heedless
  Of what their end may be.
They search the tattered rigging,
  They climb the quivering mast,
And life after life is rescued
  Till the frail ship sinks at last.

The thunderous clouds have vanished,
  And rose-fingered morn awakes,
While over the breast of ocean
  The shimmering sunlight breaks;
And the Life Brigade have finished
  The work God gave them to do,
Their names are called. "Any missing?"
  Mournful the answer,—"Two!"

Two of the best and bravest
  Have been dragged by the cruel waves
Down to the depths unmeasured,
  'Mid thousands of sailor graves!
Two lives are given for many!
  And the tears of sorrow shed,
Should be tears of joy and glory
  For the grandeur of the dead!
                    —*Minnie Mackay.*

THE END.

www.ingramcontent.com/pod-product-compliance
Lightning Source LLC
Chambersburg PA
CBHW031246260626
47169CB00007B/2472